Kidnap!

FIONA KELLY

Catnip

i

CATNIP BOOKS
Published by Catnip Publishing Ltd.
Islington Business Centre
3-5 Islington High Street
London N1 9LQ

This edition published 2007
1 3 5 7 9 10 8 6 4 2

Create by Ben M. Baglio
London W6 0HE

A CIP catalogue record for this book is available from the British Library

ISBN 978-1-84647-031-8

Printed in Poland

www.catnippublishing.co.uk

1

The Face at the Window

Amy Hunt started to laugh. 'A magic set? A top hat and wand and everything? Jamie? You're kidding!'

Her best friend, Holly Adams, made a face. 'There's some good tricks in it. It's not bad.'

'What isn't?' Josh Hamilton, last of the trio, came up behind them, chewing an apple.

'Hi, Josh! Where have you been all lunch-time – car-spotting as usual? Jamie got a magic set for his birthday!' Amy was chortling.

'Jamie doing magic?' Josh snorted. 'He's all thumbs!'

'He's driving us nuts trying out all the tricks,'

Holly told him. 'They keep going wrong.'

Amy poked her in the ribs. 'And I bet you help them!'

Holly had to laugh. She shrugged, admitting, 'Sometimes! Well, you can't let little brothers think they know it all!'

'Sabotage!' Amy guffawed. Everybody round them winced and moved away. Amy was the smallest and youngest of the three, but her laugh was the loudest in the whole Thomas Petheridge Comprehensive School.

'I'll show you some of the tricks in the booklet, if you like,' Holly offered. 'How to stick a pin in a balloon—'

'Anybody can do *that*!' Amy protested.

'Without popping it?'

Holly's friends considered it for a moment. 'That's different,' Josh admitted.

'Or how to make an egg balance on its end.'

Josh stuck his apple in his mouth to let his hands move freely as he imagined the egg, poised on one end, rolling . . . 'Can't—'

He spluttered, and took the apple out again. Amy laughed even louder.

'Can't be done,' he said when he could speak

clearly. 'Unless you put a pile of salt on the table – is that it?'

'No. Hard table, no props of any kind, don't break the egg! Even the K.I.D.Z. couldn't solve this puzzle!'

'You wanna bet?' Amy asked.

'We can solve any mystery!' Josh boasted.

It was just about true. The three youngsters were the K.I.D.Z., and had solved several crimes in their area. It had started out as a kind of joke; just Amy and Holly, banding together to copy the exploits of the heroine of their favourite book, *Harriet the Spy*. But when Josh had joined them, just in time to foil a bank robbery, the newspaper reports had called them the K.I.D.Z., and the name had stuck.

'Remember the forgers?' Amy demanded.

'And the mystery shoes?' Josh nodded. 'We'll find the answer to this one, too!'

'Yeah!' Amy nodded. 'It's about time another mystery came up. I'm getting bored!'

Holly laughed. 'Do you want to try it tonight? I'll come home with you, Amy, and watch you tear your hair out.'

Grimacing, Amy shook her head. 'I'm going to the dentist straight after school. I'll come round to your house about six o'clock, and you can help me with my French homework.'

Holly grinned. 'I'd rather do ten lots of French than go to the dentist! There's the bell. See you later!'

She waved and went off to join her class.

'I'll come round about six, too,' Josh said to Amy as he tossed his apple core in a bin and picked up his case. 'See you then!'

To her annoyance, Amy needed two fillings that afternoon. Rubbing the numb side of her face, she decided to buy herself a Mars Bar. Defiance to dentists!

She cycled briskly from the surgery towards the shops on Bairdshill Road, a bit off her direct route home.

She didn't often come this way, it was too hilly for easy cycling. Orangery Crescent was a pleasant street, with lots of trees and bushes in the gardens of big detached houses set back off the road, with curved drives leading up to their front doors.

The only thing wrong with it, she thought, was

the wasps. They were everywhere. It had been a very hot summer, and the air was so full of flying insects that she had to cycle along with her mouth shut. She didn't want to swallow a wasp, she thought, trying not to grin.

Suddenly there was a tremendous crash. Amy slammed on her brakes and looked back. A girl with short dark-red hair was standing at the first-floor window of a house to her left. Glass was still tinkling down on to the drive below.

The girl reached up unsteadily to hold the window-sash as if for support.

'Are you all right?' Amy called up to her. She propped her bike against the garden wall, shoved the squeaky gate open and started to run up the drive towards the house.

The girl's mouth opened and shut. 'What was that?' Amy called.

She heard only a startled cry as a big man gripped the girl's shoulder and pulled her back out of sight before leaning out of the broken window and glaring at Amy.

'What do you want? Go away!' he shouted down.

'I just came in to see if your daughter was all

right,' Amy said. Behind him, she could just see other people moving in the room. The girl was weeping.

'Did you break the window?' the man demanded. He looked furious.

'Me?' Amy was indignant. 'Of course not! Look, all the glass is out here!' She pointed to the splinters and lumps of glass scattered over the gravel. 'It was your daughter who broke it. Has she cut herself?'

The girl had stopped crying. The man seemed to get a grip on his temper. He smiled tightly down at Amy.

'No, no. She's all right,' he called. 'She tripped. She has dizzy turns. It's the heat. She's OK. You don't need to worry. You can go away now. Goodbye.' He stood watching until Amy turned back to her bike.

What a nasty man! Amy thought. She hoped the girl was all right. Maybe she wasn't his daughter. Maybe he'd been trying to kill her, to throw her out of the window, and only Amy's arrival had stopped him! Or maybe – maybe she was letting her fantasies run on a bit too much!

That evening Amy and Josh tried a hundred times to stand an egg on end on Holly's kitchen table.

'Oh, no! That's the third one we've broken – sorry!' Josh swept another burst egg into a bowl and wiped up.

'Scrambled eggs for breakfast tomorrow!' Holly's mother was sitting by the table, laughing at them.

'Do you know how to do it, Mrs Adams?' Amy asked.

'Oh, yes,' she told them. 'It's very simple – like knitting.'

'I don't think knitting's simple!' Amy complained. 'I tried to do a scarf once, and the feet came out different sizes!'

She guffawed again as they all made faces at her.

'OK, Holly, I give up!' Josh said. 'How do you do it?'

Holly raised her eyebrows snootily. 'Told you you wouldn't get it! Give up, Amy?'

Amy shrugged. 'Oh, I suppose so!'

'OK, give me an egg.' Holly turned it point

up and gently tap-tap-tapped the blunt end on the table. 'There's a little air-bubble in here,' she explained. 'And it's held by a kind of skin inside, so you can just dent the end – there it goes!' The end of the egg crumpled, very slightly.

She balanced the egg on the tiny flat bit and stood back in triumph. 'Da-naah! No props, and it's not broken!'

Mrs Adams chuckled at the disgusted expression on Josh and Amy's faces. 'Easy when you know how,' she said.

Jamie bounced in, wearing a short black velvet cloak and a top-hat, and brandishing a handful of cards. 'Are you ready for my latest trick?' he demanded. 'Pick a card!'

Mrs Adams hastily stood up. 'I'll go and watch the news, and leave you to it.'

'Better get it over and done with,' Josh said, under his breath. Resigned, he took a card. 'Ten of clubs.'

'You're not supposed to tell me!' Jamie screwed up his face. 'Pick another one, and this time don't say!'

'OK, OK.' This time, Josh picked the five of diamonds. 'What next?'

Jamie was sneaking a look at the next card up. 'Put it back now. And then I'll tell you which one it was! I'm magic! I'm the magickest ever!'

'Why were little brothers ever invented?' Holly sighed.

Josh couldn't resist it. While Jamie wasn't watching, he put the card back, but not in the same place he'd got it from. 'Now what?'

Jamie stacked the cards on the kitchen table. 'Abracadabra!' he shouted, waving his hands in a magical way.

'Hocus, pocus, diplodocus!' Amy suggested, winking at Josh.

'Oh, shut up!' Jamie snapped. He turned the cards over on to the table, one by one, until he came to the card he'd looked at, and pounced on the next. 'Got it! King of clubs!'

Serious-faced, Josh shook his head. 'Five of diamonds.'

Jamie's grin disappeared. 'It can't have been!'

'It was. I saw it.' Holly patted Jamie's head consolingly. 'Maybe you'd better read the instructions again.'

Jamie's face crumpled up. 'But I did it right!' he yelled in frustration.

Josh grinned. 'The quickness of the hand deceives the eye,' he said.

Jamie glowered at him. 'You did it! You cheated!' His lower lip stuck out.

'With that cloak and hat, and that face, you look like Dracula in a temper!' Amy started to laugh even louder. 'Hey, what do you get if you cross Dracula and a hot dog?' she demanded.

They all looked at her. 'Is this another of your rotten jokes for *The Tom-tom*?' Josh asked.

Amy helped Holly edit the school magazine, and often tried out her contributions to the bad-jokes page on her friends.

Now, she giggled. 'Could be! Well? What do you get if you cross Dracula—'

'And a hot dog?' Jamie had lost his pout. 'Dunno. What?'

'A fangfurter!'

They all booed.

Suddenly, from the living-room, Mrs Adams called them. 'Hey, you lot! Come through – quick!' They all looked at one another. What could be so exciting?

Mrs Adams scarcely glanced round as they came in. 'Highgate's on the news!'

On the television a young man was being interviewed. 'I was delivering a load of paper in the van, but the office was shut. It was lunch-time, not a soul about, see? So I got out my sandwiches, just as that car passed me, heading into the estate. And then a bike whipped out of a side passage, just over there—' He pointed, and the camera panned round to show a yellow car with a bicycle lying half under it.

'That's the Industrial Estate near the school!' Josh said. 'Holly, record this so that we can watch it again!'

'What's happened?' Holly asked, grabbing the video control.

The young man was still talking. 'The bike went right under the car, but the guy jumped off before it hit, see? So the car stopped – well, wouldn't you? And the driver, a girl, got out. And I was undoing my seatbelt to go and help, see, and then a blue car whizzed up past me, and three men jumped out, and the man off the bike jumped up, and they all grabbed the girl and shoved her in the car, see, and it was off before I could get out of the van.'

'Kidnap!' Amy gasped. 'A case for the K.I.D.Z.!'

'A big one!' Josh added.

'And right on our doorstep!' Holly was as excited as her friends.

A policeman appeared. 'The kidnappers' car was an electric blue Ford Mondeo.' One flashed on to the screen. 'Mr Kennedy states that the registration number began with an L. A blue Mondeo with the registration L426 PQZ was stolen last week, and has since been found abandoned in a deserted area of Hounslow.'

'Wowee!' Holly shouted excitedly. 'Josh, you were out spotting your car numbers at lunch-time, weren't you? At last, here's a reason for that daft hobby of yours! Did you see it?'

Josh was frowning. 'I don't remember. I'd need to check my notebook.'

Collecting car registration numbers was Josh's hobby. He had notebooks full of them, and a complete record on his father's computer.

'Anyone who has seen this car at any time during the past week, and especially today, should contact the police incident room,' said the policeman. The number flashed up.

The screen showed policemen searching among the workshops, and focused on one doorway.

'Eighteen-year-old Lucy Ogilvie had an appointment for a sitting here, with the talented young sculptor Bill Gibbs, who is carving a portrait bust of her,' the reporter said.

The half-finished carving appeared, a girl's head and shoulders in dark wood, then the picture changed to that of a red-haired girl. 'No ransom demand has yet been received by Miss Ogilvie's father, one of the partners in the merchant bank of Immington and Ogilvie. He has offered a reward of £50,000 for information that leads to the safe return of his daughter.'

The newscaster went on to talk about a fire in Newcastle.

'If we could find her, that would be a real boost for the K.I.D.Z.!' Holly said.

'And for your bank balances,' Mrs Adams agreed.

'What have we got to go on?' Holly asked. 'The car – what's wrong, Amy?'

Amy was staring at the set. Her face was red with excitement.

'Holly, play the tape back. Rewind to the girl's face, please,' she said.

'Why?' asked Holly, doing it. 'There you are.'

'Now pause it.' Amy stared at the screen. 'I – yes, I'm sure it was! It was her!'

'What?' Mrs Adams demanded. 'You think you've seen her?'

'Yes! This afternoon! At five o'clock!' Amy looked triumphant and scared at the same time. 'In a house in Orangery Crescent! I'm sure it was her!'

There was a chorus of astonishment. 'You're sure?' 'You didn't!' 'Are you certain?'

'Quiet!' Mrs Adams's voice shut them all up. 'Let's not go off half-cocked. Now, Amy, what happened?'

Amy described the girl breaking the window. 'And the man didn't even look down at the broken glass, or ask her how she was, or anything. He just chased me away.'

'You're absolutely positive it was her, Amy?'

'I'm sure!' Amy nodded hard. 'Her hair was short and curly, not long like in the picture, but it was the same colour – that dark red. And she looked ill—'

'As if she'd been hit!' Josh suggested.

'Or drugged!' Holly put in.

Mrs Adams finally nodded decisively. 'Fair enough. It might not be – but then again, it might. Hand me the phone, Holly!'

2

The Raid

Inspector Ross arrived at the Adams's house very quickly indeed. He took Amy carefully through her story several times, and was impressed by how clearly she recalled the details.

'How tall was the man?' he asked.

Amy screwed up her face, picturing the scene in her mind. 'His head was above the frame of the bottom half of the window,' she said. 'He'd be about as tall as you.'

'Could you see his hair?'

'Oh, yes. He came right up to the window. It was dark brown,' Amy said confidently. 'Going a bit grey at the edges. It was longish at the back, I think, for an older man, anyway.'

'Older?' The Inspector looked up from his notebook. 'How old?'

'About fifty,' said Amy. 'And he was thickset – not fat, but solid.'

'What was he wearing?'

'A cream shirt with darker stripes. The sleeves were rolled up. But he didn't have any tattoos.' Amy was quite disappointed about that. *The Case of the Tattooed Kidnapper* would have made a great title for a mystery!

The Inspector nodded, writing busily. 'How tall was the girl?'

'I'd say a bit taller than Holly. And her hair was that dark red, just the same as on the TV. But it was shorter; short and curly,' declared Amy.

'What was she wearing?'

'A green dress, I think. Or maybe a blouse.' To help her remember, Amy raised her arm as the girl had done. 'Yes, that's right. I couldn't see her skirt. But her arms were bare.'

The Inspector nodded. 'Right. Miss Ogilvie was wearing a green sleeveless dress. And her hair was short, like you say. It looks as if you might have found her!'

'Great!' Josh cried. He was sitting on the couch,

listening hard, while Holly took notes in a real police notebook, one of the ones the K.I.D.Z. had been given some time before when they'd helped the police solve a robbery.

Inspector Ross smiled slightly. 'Yes, the K.I.D.Z. may have done it again!'

'You know them, Inspector?' asked Mrs Adams.

He nodded. 'Inspector Simmons told me all about them. He warned me that they sometimes helped the police with their enquiries!'

'So what do we do now?' Amy asked. 'I didn't notice the number of the house. Should I take you round and show you it?'

The Inspector turned stern. 'No. You won't go near that house. Or the road at all, not anywhere along it. If you do, you may put Lucy Ogilvie's life in great danger.'

'Why?' Josh asked.

The policeman was deadly serious. 'Kidnappers are more than nervous. They're paranoid. They know that people hate kidnapping. So they're jumpy, always on the alert.'

His face was grim. 'Remember, a dead body's easier to hide from a search than someone tied up, who might manage to escape or raise the alarm.'

The K.I.D.Z. exchanged shocked looks.

Inspector Ross looked satisfied that he had impressed them. 'If the girl you saw was Lucy Ogilvie, she must have managed to slip away from them for just a few seconds. But they'll be scared now, and especially twitchy. And they got a good look at you, Amy, didn't they? And they know you saw the girl. So what will they think, if they see you driving down the road peering at the house a couple of hours later?' He shook his head. 'Even if we don't go in a police car, they might panic. And panicky people can do terrible things.'

'What will you do, then, Inspector?' Holly asked. 'Raid the house?'

Inspector Ross didn't answer her. 'Amy, what was the gateway of the house like?'

'Umm . . .' Amy thought back. 'It had big, thick posts, and a gravel drive. The gate squeaked badly.'

The Inspector nodded. 'Gravel and a squeaky gate would give warning of anybody coming in. What's the garden like?'

'It's very untidy,' she told him, 'with lots of trees and bushes that half hide the house.'

'And it'll be the only house with a broken window!' added Josh.

'Unless they've managed to get a glazier faster than I ever could,' commented Mrs Adams.

The Inspector grinned. 'True. We'll find it.' He stood up to leave.

'Will you raid it?' Amy repeated. 'Can we watch?'

He huffed. 'I thought I told you to keep right away! You've done your bit – and very well, too. We're very grateful. But now, you leave it to us. Don't interfere. If Lucy Ogilvie's there, it could be dangerous for her. We'll let you know what happens. Right?'

'Right, Inspector,' Mrs Adams said firmly. 'We understand. I'll show you out.'

The K.I.D.Z. stared at one another. 'Jackpot time, Amy!' Josh said at last. 'If it *was* her, think what we can do with the reward money! A new computer—'

'We wouldn't get a sniff of it,' Holly objected. 'Our parents would invest it all for us.'

'Oh, come on!' Amy protested. 'Not *all of it*! We'd get a choc-ice at least!'

Mrs Adams came back into the room. 'Well! Wait

till your father gets in, Holly – what an excitement to tell him about!' she said. 'I know – let's all cool down a bit with a choc-ice!'

The three K.I.D.Z. burst out laughing.

They watched and taped all the other newscasts about the kidnap, and talked so much about it, and watched the video so often, that they forgot the time. When at last Amy and Josh were ready to leave for home it was nearly ten o'clock.

In Holly's hall, they looked at each other, half-stifled with excitement.

'I wonder what's happening,' Amy said.

'Probably nothing. If they're going to make a raid, they'll leave it till about three in the morning,' Josh said. 'When everybody's asleep and slow off the mark, and they've a better chance of getting to a prisoner fast, before . . .'

'Yes.' Holly shivered, rubbing her arms, suddenly cold as she thought about Lucy Ogilvie tied up, or drugged, and helpless.

Purely by chance, of course, Josh and Amy just happened to take a route home that led in the general direction of Orangery Crescent. As they came near it, Josh said in mock surprise, 'Oh, we're quite close to that house, aren't we?'

'As if you didn't know!' Amy glanced at him sideways. 'Grove Road here's parallel to Orangery Crescent but higher up the hill. We could maybe see it between the houses here.'

'It should be safe enough to do that,' Josh said thoughtfully. 'Especially now that it's dark.'

Silently, two police vans came up behind them, and turned the corner just in front of them. Three others went on down the hill past the end of Orangery Crescent and turned in to the next road along.

Josh and Amy looked at each other. Without a word, they started to walk their bikes up Grove Road.

As Josh and Amy watched, policemen were quietly getting out of the vans and filtering into the gardens of the houses on the lower side of the road, that backed on to the kidnap house. There were no flashing lights, no shouted orders. Just men in dark clothes; some, they noted with a thrill, carrying rifles.

A policeman came over to them. 'What are you kids doing?' he asked.

'Going home,' Josh said.

The big man nodded. 'Right you are. But don't hang about. There's a gas leak round here — it might not be safe.'

They walked on. 'A gas leak? Oh well, I suppose they've got to say something to keep people away,' Amy whispered.

Two houses along, a leaning post by an open drive held an old 'For Sale' notice. Amy glanced at Josh. 'We could sneak into the garden here and watch. I don't think there's anybody living here — there are no lights or anything. Come on — you want to see as much as I do!'

He made a face. 'Yes . . . Come on, then. Just don't laugh!'

They ran their bikes into the dark drive, laid them down under a bush, and tiptoed down past the house and garage. Brick paths, not gravel, led among bushes and trees down a steep garden. They soon lost the light of the street-lamps, and had to wait for their eyes to adjust to the darkness.

'I don't like this,' Josh murmured. 'We shouldn't be here.'

Amy was too excited to stop. 'Come on. Nobody'll know!'

Doubtfully Josh followed her, creeping off the path to crouch behind some bushes clustered in the corner of the rickety fence.

'That's it, I think. That one along a bit. Yes, that's it.' Amy pointed down and across the slope.

The kidnap house stuck out from the hillside, with a path leading past the back door in a kind of cutting. Its garden fell steeply in narrow terraces, with scraggly fir trees round the edges that would screen the house from neighbours' windows above and to the sides. But from where Josh and Amy crouched, they could peer down through the lower branches on to the back door, the gate and part of the curving front drive.

'Look!' Josh pointed. Policemen were sliding among the trees and bushes, only the faintest of rustles and twitch of twigs showing where they were moving through the dark.

More men came silently down the path behind Josh and Amy and climbed cautiously over the fence into the garden below, next door to the kidnap house. Then there was stillness again.

'What happens if you're right?' Amy breathed in Josh's ear. 'If they wait till the middle of the night? How do we get out without them seeing us?'

'Tough!' he whispered back. 'You should have thought of that before. This was your idea. I'm not—' He stopped.

A man was brushing through the bushes. He paused just above them.

A deep murmur came from the tall black figure. ' "A" team?'

A tiny, tinny voice answered, 'Ready.'

' "B" team? "C" team?'

'Ready – Ready.'

The man adjusted something on his face, and stepped sideways, right on to Amy's hand.

'Ow!' It was only a whisper, but the man heard it.

He jumped, bent, snatched at whoever was there, caught Amy's long fair hair and hauled her up.

'You!' It was Inspector Ross. 'Two of you! I said—' He stopped himself. 'Stay there. Don't move an inch!' He drew a deep breath. 'Right,' he said into his radio. 'Go-go-go!'

All the street and house lights went off.

Burning with shame, but still desperate to watch, Josh and Amy froze.

Still there was no noise. A dozen men raced down the terraces of the kidnap house. Others appeared, flitting across the road below and up the drive. There was a crack at the back door, and the group of men gathered there suddenly disappeared.

'We're in!' a tinny voice reported.

'Lights! Sound!' Inspector Ross snapped into his radio.

Amy and Josh flinched, and Amy yelped again as huge floodlights suddenly dazzled the whole street. They didn't notice that all the lights had come back on in the house; they were blinking, blinded, covering their eyes. Sirens wailed and shrieked, stunning them with noise.

Above them, Inspector Ross pushed his dark goggles into place and leaned down over them again. 'I'll be back,' he yelled over the din. 'If I don't find you right here, you'll be charged with obstructing the police. Right?' He didn't wait for an answer, but vaulted the fence and hurried down to the house.

Inside, there was some shouting. Someone screamed. But there were no shots.

Then the loudspeakers stopped. Policemen came out of the house, and started searching all round it with torches, lighting up the few shadows left by the huge floodlights. They went into the shed several times, up and down the garden terraces, even probed the ground under the trees.

After a long time, the floodlights went out. The police appeared again, not triumphantly helping a girl out to the ambulance that had driven up to the front door; not carrying out a body. Just walking out, climbing back up the steps through the terraces, tramping out to the vans and cars now parked at the front. 'Oh, well. Better luck next time,' one man was saying as he climbed the fence just along from the youngsters.

'It wasn't her.' Josh's glare was hidden by the dark, but Amy could still feel it. 'All this fuss, and getting us into trouble with the police, and it wasn't her!'

'Well, I thought it was!' Amy protested. She felt sick.

Inspector Ross came out of the house and stood under the intruder light by the back door, talking to a big man. 'That's the man at the window!' Amy said, pointing. But he wasn't being arrested.

The Inspector climbed up the steps through the garden terraces and leaned over the fence to look down at them. They shrank, inside.

Josh stood up, creaking with stiffness. 'I'm sorry, sir,' he said firmly. However angry he felt with Amy, he had to back her up now. 'We all thought Amy was right. And we didn't mean to get in your way, or take any risks – we wouldn't have gone any closer . . .' His voice ran down.

The tall policeman glared down at them, his eyes gleaming in the street-lights. 'Right,' he said grimly. 'First of all, I listened carefully to what you told me, Amy. As soon as I got back to the station I sent a couple of plain-clothes men to watch the house, to see that nobody was removed from it while I checked. The estate agents told me that the tenant here just moved in a fortnight ago. A Mr Arnold Gillingham. He paid cash to rent the house for three months. That's how kidnappers would have done it. There were no references, and one or two other suspicious things. So I got a warrant and set up a raid.'

He gestured down at the house. 'The house has burglar alarms, so there was no way to get in stealthily; it had to be a big blast. Thirty men, four lighting units, loudspeaker vans. The electricity turned off in the whole street for a minute. Every household for half a mile disturbed. Old and sick people, children, babies, wakened, startled, scared.'

He waved a hand round to where the vans

and ambulance were starting to drive away. 'You watched it. We searched the house thoroughly, and the garden. We found nothing. No trace of Lucy Ogilvie, or anything else wrong.'

The Inspector's voice grew even grimmer. 'The girl you saw was Mr Gillingham's daughter, Samantha. We met her. She dyed her hair last week, disliked it, and was actually washing it out when we broke in. Maybe you heard her screaming?'

He waited till they nodded before he went on. 'She told us how she broke the window – she felt faint, staggered and put her elbow through it. She showed me the green T-shirt she'd been wearing. Everything that you saw was true – but it was all innocent.'

He half turned to glance back down the slope. 'She remembers you. So does her father. He's been very reasonable about the whole affair. He asked me to tell you he understands you thought you were helping Lucy Ogilvie, but he hopes you'll keep a stricter control on your imagination in future.'

He paused, and turned back to the youngsters. 'And frankly, so do I. You did the right thing, by telling me what you saw. So I'll take no action about you breaking my instructions, and risking hurt to Lucy Ogilvie by interfering here. You can figure for yourselves how you'd have felt if you'd been right, and had alerted the kidnappers, and Lucy Ogilvie had been killed before we reached her. But you'd be well advised to keep your mind on your school work and off rewards in future, and not bother me again. Now go home, both of you!'

Without another word, he turned and walked back down towards the house.

'That's not fair!' Amy whispered. 'He thinks I exaggerated it, just to get the reward! But I was trying to help! And I had good reason to think she was here. Everyone thought so!'

'Yes. OK. Come on. Our parents will be worried about us.' Josh could sympathise with her, but for the moment all he wanted to do was get out of there, get home, and forget all about the most embarrassing moment of his life.

3

Apologies

At school next day, of course, Holly wanted to know all about it. She had heard the sirens, and the raid had been on the morning news. But neither Josh nor Amy wanted to talk about it.

When eventually Holly did worm the story out of them, she was shocked. 'Amy! Going anywhere near there, when you knew what might happen! How could you let her, Josh?'

'I didn't twist Josh's arm or hold a gun on him!' Amy protested.

'I should have had more sense.' Josh was still feeling rotten.

'Yes, you should,' Holly told him firmly. 'You know what Amy's like—'

'Hey!' Amy was hurt. 'Stop talking about me as if I'm not here! You thought it could be her – you agreed to tell the police. You were as excited as me! Josh agreed to go up the road, and into the garden – it's not all my fault!'

Her face was red and upset, and she turned away angrily and stomped off down the corridor. 'And I won't have you lecturing me! It's not fair!' she called over her shoulder.

Holly and Josh looked at each other. At last Holly shrugged. 'Fair enough,' she said. 'It wasn't all her. We all thought she was right – and OK, I'd probably have wanted to go and watch too. I don't know that I'd actually—'

'Oh, stop it, Holly!' said Josh. 'Dad was mad that I was late home last night without warning him, and when I explained about going to look at the kidnap house and getting involved in the raid he said that made it worse, not better. It was bad enough last night, without you starting again this morning. I know how Amy feels! Leave it, will you? Please?'

They stood in dismal silence for a minute. The bell rang for the first class. Holly made a resigned face. 'See you at break?'

He shrugged. 'OK.' He really didn't feel like talking about it any more.

At break, when he and Holly arrived in the corner of the hall where they usually stood, Holly realised to her relief that he didn't look as glum. She grinned at him. 'So what do we do now?' she asked. 'Forget it? Or try to solve it?'

'You mean get the K.I.D.Z. working properly on this kidnapping?' said Josh.

'From scratch! Start all over again,' Holly nodded hopefully. 'We can't let it beat us!'

'Well,' he said thoughtfully, 'I'm grounded for a week, but I suppose we could manage. But what about Amy?'

Holly was looking past him. 'Oh, that'll be OK,' she said with a smile.

He turned round.

Amy was walking towards them, her hands full of choc-ices from the tuck-shop. She offered them one each. 'Here. Sorry I blew up like that,' she said. 'I had to tell Mum and Dad why I was late, and they read the riot act to me for ages last night, and then when you started as well, it just got to me. I'm sorry. I feel bad, but that's no reason for taking it out on you two. Have a choc-ice.'

She giggled. 'Why did the soprano ghost live in the freezer?'

Holly sighed. 'Go on, then. Why did the soprano ghost live in the freezer?'

'To give people ice-creams! High screams – get it?'

'Oh, no!' Josh and Holly rolled their eyes at Amy as she guffawed; but they all cheered up.

Holly nibbled all the chocolate off her choc-ice first, before eating the ice-cream. Josh took bites, as if he was eating a sandwich, and chewed it. Amy always bit off a corner, stuck her tongue in and tried to lick out the ice cream without breaking the rest of the chocolate shell. She never managed it; this time, as usual, it melted in her hand before she could get much out, and she ended up licking a sticky mess off her fingers and wrists and the inside of the paper wrapper.

'Come round to my house tonight after school?' Josh suggested. 'We'll start a real investigation into the kidnapping. I've got a couple of ideas—'

'So have I,' added Holly.

Amy looked at them in surprise. 'But we *know* where Lucy is. In that house.'

'Come on, Amy!' exclaimed Holly. 'The police

looked everywhere. You even watched them do it. I'd have thought you'd have given up on that idea!'

Slowly Amy shook her head. 'No. I saw her. I looked at her picture again on the morning newscast, and it was definitely her.'

Holly rolled her eyes in despair, but Amy ploughed on. 'Do you remember what the Inspector said the girl in the house said she was wearing, Josh?'

Josh thought back. 'A T-shirt. A green T-shirt.'

'Right. But the girl I saw was wearing a sleeveless top. I've been thinking about it. It came just to here.' She showed them with a finger where the edge of the sleeve had been, right on the point of her shoulder. 'It wasn't a T-shirt,' she insisted. '*So* Miss Greenham—'

'Gillingham,' Josh said.

'Whatever, was lying. *So* they must be involved. *So* we have to go back to that house.'

Holly and Josh exchanged glances. 'Well, maybe Inspector Ross made a mistake about what she said,' said Josh.

'Or she called it a T-shirt and he just copied her,' Holly suggested.

'Look, the police gave the house a thorough

search, Amy.' Josh shrugged. 'You can't get away from that. Lucy Ogilvie wasn't there.'

It made no difference. Amy just looked stubborn. 'She was. I saw her.'

Holly rolled her eyes at Josh. Amy could be so stubborn!

They argued about it again at lunch-time, and before they went home after school. 'Look, if we're going to take on this case we have to do it properly,' said Holly.

'Yes! So we should watch the house,' Amy insisted.

At last Josh lost patience. 'Look, will you stop going on about that house!' he snapped. 'You just hate being wrong! Forget it!'

'No!' Amy snarled back at him. 'I saw Lucy there! And I don't care what you two do – *I'm* going to investigate the house. It's the best clue we've got! I *know* I saw her there! If you don't believe me, you can go and boil your heads! Both of you!'

Furious, Amy stormed off to get her bike.

'Oh, dear!' Holly sighed. 'She really has got a bee in her bonnet about that house!'

Josh made a face. 'Well, we can't go near there

– not after the police and all the disturbance. Come round tonight, Holly, and we'll talk it over.'

Holly nodded. 'OK, I'll be round about six. I'll give Amy a ring – maybe she'll have calmed down by then.'

But when she phoned the Hunts' house that evening, before going over to Josh's, it was Amy's older sister Becky who answered. She sounded puzzled. 'Isn't Amy with you? She went out at five, saying she had some detecting to do. Mum and Dad are fizzing at her for all that bother last night. They warned her if she caused any more trouble they'd stop her pocket money for a month, and she has to be back in by eight at the latest.'

'Maybe she's gone straight round to Josh's,' said Holly. 'Thanks, Becky. See you!' She made a face to herself. She bet she knew where Amy was! Hidden in the garden above the mysterious house.

Holly was almost right. At that moment. Amy

was actually walking up the drive of the house in Orangery Crescent.

She had considered it all day, very seriously, without even thinking of any jokes.

If these Gillingham people were in fact kidnappers, she mustn't alarm them any more. But she had to get close up to the house, recall what had happened, and either convince herself that her friends were right, and she'd exaggerated what she thought she'd seen, or reassure herself that she had made no mistake.

Maybe she could find some clues that would convince the others, too.

But how could she do it?

At last it came to her. Simple! She'd go and apologise.

As Amy pushed the gate open, it squeaked. *I remember that,* she thought. *It's not a clue, but at least I got something right!*

There was a man repairing the big first-floor window. 'Hi!' He grinned cheerily down at Amy. He turned to speak to someone inside. 'Hey, miss, you've got a visitor!'

A tall girl appeared behind the glazier. 'I'll come down,' she said, and turned away.

Amy stood waiting for her to open the door.

This was where she had stood yesterday, in a lake of broken glass. Most of it had been cleared away, but gleams in the gravel showed where some was still lying about.

Something odd about one bit caught Amy's eye. She picked it up, and stuck it in her pocket as the door opened.

The young woman who stood there was quite tall and solidly built, with a wide face and big round eyes. She was about twenty years old. Her brown hair was short and curly, with traces of red at the roots. This must be the Samantha Gillingham Inspector Ross had spoken to.

Amy heaved a sigh of relief. She'd never seen this girl before in her life. She certainly wasn't the girl who had broken the window.

'Yes?' Samantha said. 'What do you want?' There was a wariness about her, a stiffness in the way she stood, as if she was ready for trouble.

Amy bit her lip. She had to convince Samantha she didn't suspect her. 'I'm – I came to apologise.'

'What for?' The young woman's shoulders relaxed a touch, but she frowned.

'For thinking you were the girl that was kidnapped.'

Amy could see Samantha start, and then relax. 'Oh, that was you, was it? I didn't recognise you. But I wasn't feeling so good yesterday. And then last night – it was you who called the police, wasn't it?'

Her face changed to anger, but from a kind of sly satisfaction in the woman's eyes, Amy was sure it was acting. 'What a shock! The lights went off, and then the din gave me the fright of my life! And the police burst in on me when I was washing my hair. I thought it was terrorists. And it was you who did it!'

'I'm terribly sorry,' Amy repeated.

'Fancy thinking I was kidnapped, just because I broke a window!' Samantha's eyes were sharp on Amy all the time to see how she was taking it. 'I felt dizzy, and I staggered, and next thing I knew my elbow was through the glass. I was lucky I didn't cut my arm off.' Her eyes narrowed tensely. 'You remember me?'

Amy thought fast. 'I broke my glasses a couple of days back.' She didn't wear glasses, of course, but Samantha wouldn't know that. 'That's why I thought you looked like the girl on the news. Now I see you close up, I can see you aren't really like her. It was just the hair colour. Like I said, I'm so sorry for causing all the upset.'

To her satisfaction, Samantha looked pleased. 'Well, Dad says you were just doing the right thing. But please don't do it again – not without warning us first! Goodbye!'

Amy was quite happy to smile as if she was glad the woman was taking it so well. She'd got what she wanted! She walked back to her bike and rode off, while Samantha smiled and waved triumphantly from the top of the steps.

Round the corner, Amy stopped. What now? Did she have enough to go to the others with? No, not yet. She made a face. She'd show them!

She turned her bike uphill, and then into Grove Road again. Yes, the 'For Sale' house, the garden of which they'd gone into yesterday, was still deserted. She stopped, fiddled with her pedals for a second while a car went past, checked that nobody was watching, and ran her bike into the drive. There was a corner by the back door where she could hide it.

Even if the others wouldn't help, she could watch the house alone!

She scurried down the garden. The bushes of the

night before were laurels, whose heavy leaves would hide her completely. No thorns, thank goodness! She could see well, through the rails of the fence and the scraggly fir trees. She was only about twenty metres from the house corner, a perfect spy hideout. Harriet the Spy herself couldn't have hoped for better!

There were four windows looking out this way, on to the steep terraces behind the house. They were all blank; only one had curtains, and one a drawn blind. Nothing was moving, except the wasps. Dozens of them. Amy shivered.

Nothing moved in the house below. Nothing at all.

It was almost boring.

Amy imagined the girl above her at the window yesterday, and then the woman today. *Yes, Samantha Gillingham is a good bit taller,* she thought. *And she's heavier built. But that's just my own memory, not proof – not solid evidence.*

After what seemed like hours, her legs got stiff, and she moved to ease them. Something jabbed her hip. Suddenly she remembered the odd bit of glass she'd picked up from the drive, and fished it out of her pocket. It was a small chunky piece, not flat but thick and solid, and definitely green, with a rounded side; not window glass, for sure.

She thought back. *I was on the drive, just down there. Glass was all round my feet, I couldn't help standing on it. And it was bumpy!*

Samantha had said she broke the window with her elbow. But there had been lumps of glass on the drive too, thick chunks of curvy green glass like this, not just flat plates.

Amy grinned in triumph. This glass was from an ash-tray or a vase, something like that, heavy enough to break the window, but not too big or heavy to move. It could have been thrown through the window to call for help. *This* was real proof! Holly and Josh would have to listen to her now.

Below Amy, the back door of the house in Orangery Crescent opened. Samantha Gillingham came out carrying a bag of rubbish. A movement-activated security light came on. She looked all round, staring out into the garden.

Amy suddenly felt scared; what if Samantha saw her? The sun was shining right at her. The bushes hid her from the back, but in front, were the trees and the fence really thick enough to hide her completely? She felt her heart thumping.

After a minute, the young woman opened the dustbin by the door, and dropped in the bag. The light went off. The woman didn't go right back inside. She stood on the narrow concrete path that ran along the back of the house, breathing deeply, enjoying the coolness in the shade behind the house. Then she started picking some flowers from the lowest terrace.

There was a tickle on Amy's forearm. She glanced down, and stiffened; a wasp was crawling along her arm!

She couldn't move, or she'd be seen. She blew at the wasp. But it didn't fly away. It crawled down to her wrist, and started to lick at her skin.

It was licking at a spot of sweetness left over from her melted choc-ice earlier.

She watched in fascinated fright as it finished. Then it rose into the air and flew off. Phew!

By this time Samantha had gathered a bunch of flowers. She straightened, stretched, and looked round keenly again before she went back to the door. The security light came on just as she reached the door and went inside.

Amy eyed the dustbin. There might be a clue in there. In the K.I.D.Z.'s favourite television programme, *Spyglass,* the best clues were often found in waste-bins. There couldn't be much to rake through; the bins had been emptied only yesterday.

Her parents hadn't wanted to let her come out at all, and had threatened battle, murder and sudden death if she was home later than eight. She checked her watch. It was half past seven already.

Oh, well, she thought, I'll just have to risk it. Getting proof that could save a girl from kidnappers is more important than getting into trouble!

4

Deductions

Josh's house had a small boxroom that the K.I.D.Z. used as their office. They had a big street map of London pinned to one wall, with pins in it to show where they'd been involved in solving crimes. Now, after finishing their homework, Holly and Josh were sitting at the desk trying to make sense of the kidnap case.

Holly had her notebook out again. She tapped it with her pen.

'Right. I'll make a proper Crime Report.' She wrote the heading, "KIDNAPPING – LUCY OGILVIE". 'Josh, put a pin in the map to show where it happened. No – use the red ones for a case in progress. Now, let's get it all down.'

She noted everything that had been on the news programmes. 'Banker's daughter. Pots of money, I suppose.'

Josh snorted. 'It's not much good kidnapping poor people!'

'No, I suppose not,' agreed Holly. She went on writing. 'Yellow car . . . bike . . . van. It was unlucky for the kidnappers that the kidnapping was seen, wasn't it? What was his name, Josh?'

'The van driver? Mr Kennedy,' Josh told her. He was frowning as he studied the map.

'I don't understand one or two things about this,' he muttered, to himself as much as to Holly. 'Inspector Ross said that kidnappers are paranoid about taking precautions. So why did they risk being seen? The van wasn't thirty metres away. Why go ahead, with a witness there? Lucy went there every week, didn't she? The sculptor – Gibbs, wasn't it? – said so last night on TV.'

'How did they know when?' wondered Holly. 'Was it a regular appointment, or did she just come when he needed her?' She noted that in the "Find Out" column. 'The kidnappers had to know when she'd be there, to set up the bike accident to stop her.'

'Right,' agreed Josh. 'How did they find out? But I still don't understand why they went for her with the van there. Next time there might not have been anybody there at all.'

"Maybe they didn't know the driver was in it,' said Holly. She stopped writing to think about it. 'He was having his lunch break, eating his sandwiches. The van would have been parked for a while. And there aren't any other units along that particular bit of road, are there? They'd think the place was deserted.'

'Maybe. But I don't know. He said he saw the accident – well, the bike going under the car – but he couldn't get out in time to help.' Josh shook his head. 'I don't see it.'

He sat down in a chair and started to act it out. 'Look. I'm in my van. I see the car go by, and the bike, and the accident. Crash! OK. The girl stops, and gets out of her car. That takes about five seconds. The kidnap car drives up, and the men get out, and drag her into it, and get away. That's another five or six seconds, at the very least. More like ten, probably. Well, you can do a lot even in five seconds, never mind fifteen. You can certainly get out of a van. All you have to do is open the

47

door and jump out.' He opened a pretend door and stood up. 'See! It only takes two seconds!'

He had his seat-belt on,' said Holly. 'He said so.'

'While he was eating?' Josh asked. 'Think about it. He'd arrived during the lunch break – but he must have got out to check that the door was locked. There could have been a secretary, a porter, somebody about. So, if he'd been out, why would he fasten his seat-belt again? He knew he'd be getting out again as soon as somebody arrived.'

Holly looked thoughtful. 'That's true. Maybe he just did it out of habit? But yes, it is odd.'

'It is indeed.' Josh picked up another pin. 'Where's the old railway siding where that Mondeo was found? Hounslow?' He reached up to the big map, and studied it again, frowning.

'What's wrong?' asked Holly. 'The news tonight said the car had been reported by two or three people, racing along the roads that way just after the kidnap. They must have switched cars there.'

Josh waved a hand to stop her. 'Hang on, hang on. Looking at the map now, I've just realised something. Go back a bit.'

He was tracing roads on the map. 'There are

only two exits from the industrial estate. This one takes you out on to James Street, and then you can go on any number of fairly quiet roads across the Heath towards where the car was found. See it?'

Holly nodded.

'The only other way out goes straight up on to the High Street, right here,' Josh went on, putting his finger on the place. 'And it's one-way there. They'd have to go along as far as the traffic lights, and then right down to Parliament Street before they could get off that way again.'

'The back road's more sensible. If anything went wrong, they'd be seen,' Holly commented. 'I wouldn't have risked the High Street. Especially not at lunch time – it's busy.'

'Nor me!' Josh agreed. 'It seems a silly risk to take if you don't have to. Now look, yesterday you asked me if I'd seen the car. I checked before I went to bed. I was down on the corner there, right at the traffic lights.' He was rummaging in his desk for the jotter he used to take his neat notes of the car numbers he saw, before transferring them to his father's computer.

'Here we are. Yes. Look.' He held the notebook

out to her. 'That's when I started, at twelve thirty-four – and the kidnap was at about ten to one. And I stopped at ten past, to get back to school.'

Holly looked down the long list. 'Did I say busy? This looks as if it was jam-packed! Yes – there it is! That's the Mondeo's number!'

'Yes.' Josh was grinning. 'But look at the heading. I was noting the cars on Union Street, not on the High Street itself. And I wrote down the Mondeo's number. But Union Street doesn't pass anywhere near the Industrial Estate!'

'So the car didn't come from the estate. So—'

Josh finished for her. 'The driver was lying!'

They cheered. A proper deduction, from factual evidence; this was real detecting!

'So this Kennedy man was one of the gang, and they wanted the Mondeo to be seen,' Holly said after a moment. 'Why?'

'To distract everybody,' said Josh, with certainty.

'Like Jamie's magic tricks,' Holly nodded. 'Make people look in the wrong direction.'

'Right!' Josh slapped a hand on the desk. 'They sent the big, jazzy electric blue Mondeo to make the police look west, towards the airport, away from the real kidnap car—'

'Which wasn't racing about, getting itself noticed. It was quietly driving along, well inside the speed limit, to − where?' Holly wondered. 'Somewhere close, to make the run and the risk as short as possible.'

She came over to look at the map beside Josh. 'Look. Only half a kilometre from the estate. Just along James Road, and then up Forest Road towards my house, and second right—'

'Orangery Crescent. Oh, no!' Josh rolled his eyes. 'Don't tell me Amy's right after all!'

They looked at each other for a minute in silence. 'We've got to tell the police,' said Holly.

'After yesterday?' Josh put his head in his hands and groaned.

'I know! But we've *got* to!' Holly tapped Josh's notebook. 'It's new evidence. They can't argue with the facts, written down here. This proves that the driver was in on the plan. At the very least, it's a new lead for them.'

Josh sighed. 'I agree. I'm just not looking forward to meeting Inspector Ross again! Oh, well. Come on, we'll tell Dad!'

Mr Hamilton looked at the notebook, and listened to what they had to say, and simply nodded.

'Yes, of course you must go. I'll drive you, just to be certain that Josh comes right home this time!

'You phone home, to let your parents know where you are,' he told Holly. 'We'll go and start the car.'

As Josh opened the front door, he saw a small figure pedalling furiously up the road towards them.

'That's Amy!' he said. 'Dad, something's wrong. She's supposed to be home by eight, and it's after ten to. She'll never make it.'

His father shrugged. 'Taxi service, that's me,' he said. 'I suppose her bike'll go in the boot — even if it won't shut.' He opened the boot of the car, and beckoned. 'Right, Amy,' he called. 'Pile in, I'll get you home in time.'

'No — no!' Amy puffed. 'Please can I use your phone, Mr Hamilton, to tell mum and dad I'll be late? And then will you take me to the police station, please? I've got some real clues!'

'So have we!' said Josh. 'You could be right about that house, Amy!'

'I *am* right!' she told him. 'You bet I am!'

They found everyone at the police station was busy. A lorry had shed its load of frozen fish over a crossroads, and traffic was jammed for miles. It was almost an hour before Inspector Ross had time to invite the K.I.D.Z. to come through into an interview room. He sat down wearily opposite them. 'Right. What is it this time?'

The K.I.D.Z. exchanged a glance. He was all ready to disbelieve them. But they had to go on.

Josh and Holly told their story first, and showed the policeman Josh's notebook.

The Inspector nodded. Without any comment, he turned to Amy. 'And what have you got to say today, Miss Hunt?'

'Real evidence, Inspector!' Amy declared defiantly.

She described why she was sure that the woman she'd met wasn't the same one she had seen at the window.

Holly and Josh nodded, but the Inspector looked resigned. Before he could say anything, Amy said, 'But I know that's not evidence, so I kept looking.'

She produced the bit of green glass, and explained where she'd seen it before.

Again, he opened his mouth to speak, but she kept going. 'And that's not all!'

She told them about the dustbin. 'I was terribly careful, don't worry! I crept down into the next garden, and then slipped across at the side – there's only one window there.'

The Inspector was shaking his head, but she ignored it. 'The rubbish wasn't all piled in, it was tied up in supermarket bags. Just two bags. So I took them out, one after the other, and hid round the corner while I looked in them, and tied them up again and put them back, so they wouldn't know I'd been there. One was just tins and packets of pizzas and fast food. But *this* was in the other one.' Triumphantly, she produced a flattened packet.

'What is it?' Holly asked eagerly. She poked at the packet, and her face fell. 'Hair-dye?'

'But we knew that the girl used that, Amy,' said Josh in exasperation. 'She told the Inspector that. That's not a clue!'

'Yes, it is!' Amy insisted. 'Because the bins were emptied yesterday! And she said she dyed her hair a week ago! So why wasn't the packet taken away? She can't have used it till after the bins were emptied. Not days ago like she said.'

The K.I.D.Z. looked at the detective. He had been writing down what they reported while they were talking, and now he sat back and looked at his notebook.

'Let's see if I've got this correct. Miss Adams and Mr Hamilton think the Mondeo was a decoy car; evidence: discrepancies they've noticed in the story told by the driver of the delivery van, and Mr Hamilton's car-spotter's notebook. Right?'

He picked up the notebook and sighed. 'Just how accurate is this, son?'

Josh's jaw dropped. 'I never—' He stopped, and set his jaw. 'Everything in there is true. And exactly right. Everything.'

'Times? Starting time, 12.34? Stopping time, 13.09? Is it really that accurate?'

Mr Hamilton spoke up beside his son. 'If that's what he put in, that's what it was. Josh's very reliable.'

Josh felt better. Dad believed him, anyway.

The Inspector didn't look convinced. 'Maybe your watch was wrong, son. Maybe you took down a wrong number – just one letter or number could be off.'

He smiled slightly. 'Don't get me wrong – I'm not saying you've invented it, or changed any of the numbers to fit your story. But you could have made a mistake. Nobody's perfect.'

'I'm certain I didn't.' Josh tried to sound reliable and reasonable. 'I'm always careful.'

'Do you remember the car itself?' Inspector Ross asked.

'No,' Josh had to admit. 'It was busy. Look at the list – nearly three hundred cars in thirty-five minutes. And I had no reason to be looking for that car specially. I can't recall any of them, not individually.'

'Well.' The detective shook his head. 'Now, Miss Hunt.' He turned to Amy. 'You do realise you've committed a crime?'

'What?' Amy's jaw dropped, just as Josh's had. 'But I was looking for clues – to catch a kidnapper!'

'You went into private property without a warrant, and removed belongings—'

'It was thrown out!' Amy protested. 'It was rubbish!'

'It was still theirs,' Inspector Ross said firmly. 'People change their minds, get things back out of dustbins – bills thrown away by mistake, or whatever. Until it actually leaves their ground, it belongs to them, and you've no right to touch it. You had no right to be there at all, without their permission. So it's actually burglary.'

'For an old empty packet?' Amy gasped. 'You can't be serious!'

'The police don't have the right to raid houses without a search warrant,' Inspector Ross told her. 'Not even their dustbins. So why should you?'

'To save that girl!' Holly cried. 'Don't you care about her?'

Inspector Ross's eyes glinted. He set his elbows on the desk, clasped his hands, leaned his chin on them and stared at Holly until she sank back in her chair, abashed.

'I'll forget you said that, Miss Adams,' he said grimly. 'We've got a dozen men in here, all working four or five hours unpaid overtime trying to find that girl. I've been in since seven this morning myself. We're grateful for your information, we can't do without it, but we don't ask you to come out and physically help us fight criminals. All we do ask is that you don't make life more difficult for us!'

He relaxed slightly, rubbed a hand over his tired

face and flicked his notebook with his finger. 'You admit you only saw the girl at the window for a few seconds, Miss Hunt, at a distance. You could be wrong too. It could have been Miss Gillingham, even though you don't think so.'

Amy was going to protest, but decided not to. She didn't want to risk annoying him even more, and being charged with burglary.

'The glass . . . Sorry to disappoint you,' the Inspector went on, 'but that's not a clue either. The girl could have been holding an ash-tray when she fell against the window, and simply not mentioned it. And as for the packet of hair-dye — ' He puffed gently. 'Isn't there anything in your bedroom that should have been thrown out a week ago?'

There was a silence. Then Josh nerved himself to ask, 'So you're not going to do anything?'

'What do you suggest?' Inspector Ross asked. 'There's nothing in what you've told me to make us want to go back to that house. A lot of your ideas, we're already working on — we're really not as slow as some people think. Leave your notebook, if you don't mind.' He was writing out a receipt for it as he spoke. 'Thank you. But all the rest — they're coincidences, or have other explanations. More likely ones, at that.'

The detective eyed the K.I.D.Z. sternly. 'Thank you for trying to help,' he told them. 'I won't say you're desperate to get your picture on the TV as heroes – I think you've got more sense than that. If you did get into the news just now, it would be as silly kids.'

The three K.I.D.Z. felt totally deflated.

'Maybe you just want to help too much,' he said, relaxing a bit and looking almost kindly. 'And you all have lively imaginations.'

Mr Hamilton nodded.

Inspector Ross stood up. 'Miss Hunt, don't go raking round dustbins again. Please. Leave it to us. Or you'll end up in serious trouble.'

He didn't say any more, just stood and waited.

Silently, the children and Mr Hamilton filed out.

5

A Genius-Sized Idea

Friday was usually a good day for all of them; Holly had Drama, Josh had Art, and Amy had Games, but this particular day none of them had much heart to enjoy them. It was a very subdued trio who met at break.

Josh looked at Holly's downcast face. 'Now you know how *we* felt,' he said.

She nodded. 'Yes. I wish I'd been more sympathetic yesterday.'

'We're still right, though,' said Amy. Her stubborn expression would have scared off a thunderstorm. 'I know what I saw,' she stated firmly. 'You know what you saw, Josh. Even if they don't believe us. It's not just our imaginations. It's not! We're still right.'

'Fat lot of good it does us, though,' said Holly. 'I'm in as much trouble as you two now. You should have heard Mum last night!'

'One good thing,' Josh told her. 'Dad does believe I'm telling the truth. *He's* on our side.'

'Oh, they're all on our side!' Holly exclaimed. 'They just disagree with us about how they should show it! My parents think I need to be taken in hand. I have to go straight home from school, and stay in at night as well, for a week, like you.'

She imitated the annoyance in her mother's voice. ' "Just concentrate on your school work, Holly, and no more of this detective business!" Huh! Mum practically said "this detective nonsense," but she remembered just in time that we've actually done pretty well at it!'

'At least the papers haven't printed our names, for prompting the raid,' said Josh.

'But what can we do?' Amy demanded. 'We're right!'

'Yes,' Holly said. 'We've got to do something!'

'We'll – we'll think about it,' Josh told them. He didn't know what else to say.

They sniffed in disgust. But they had no ideas, either.

'Oh, well.' Holly sighed. 'Want to slip out and come down to the shops at lunch-time? I need to get some balloons. I promised some people I'd show them that trick of Jamie's.'

Amy perked up a little. 'You mean popping balloons without popping them? Yes, how *do* you do that?'

'Come along and I'll show you,' promised Holly. 'I'm going to put an article about it in *The Tom-tom*. Puzzles, tricks – that kind of thing.'

'Hey, hands off!' Amy protested. 'You write the mystery page. Magic's more like a joke – it should be on my page, not yours.'

Josh tried to grin. 'Don't fight about it! One half of the Thomas Petheridge School magazine's editorial team assaulting the other half would certainly get into the papers, but you don't need to boost sales that way! See you at half twelve, OK?'

In the store at lunch-time, Holly dropped a small roll of Sellotape in beside the balloons in her wire basket.

'What's that for?' Amy asked.

'You'll see. Do you want an ice-cream?'

'Oh, magic!' Amy was almost cheerful again. 'Have you tried these new—'

She suddenly grabbed Josh's arm and steered him and Holly swiftly round the end of a tall stand of birthday cards.

'What is it?' asked Josh.

'Look.' Amy peeked round the end of the stand. 'That's the woman from the house. Samantha Gillingham. In the blue anorak. See her?'

Cautiously, they peered round the stand.

'What do we do?' Amy whispered.

'What do you suggest?' asked Holly. 'Just go right up to her and say, "Excuse me, have you got a kidnapped girl in your house?" Or kidnap her, and beat it out of her? What *can* we do?'

'We can follow her and see where she goes,' Josh said.

'Oh, great. Watch her buying – what is it?' Holly sneaked another glance. 'Tights here, and then round the supermarket for her weekend's shopping, or something perfectly ordinary. What would she be doing? Buying a mask and gun? Don't be silly!'

Amy bit her lip. Holly was probably right. Samantha certainly didn't seem to be doing anything suspicious at the moment. 'I think we should follow her,' she said defiantly. 'You never know. Anything could turn up!'

Josh nodded. 'I agree,' he said. 'We've got twenty minutes. We should use it as much as we can. Look – she's going to the check-out.'

Holly stiffened. 'Who's that? That man there?' A young man had moved forward from the sweet rack to stand behind Miss Gillingham in the queue. 'I know him!'

'Where have I seen him before?' Josh whispered.

'On the TV,' yelped Amy. 'He was the driver of the van! Mr Kennedy!'

'Yes!' Holly agreed. 'Yes, that's him! They're meeting! So they must be in it together! What'll we do – Amy! What are you doing? Come back!'

Amy had taken the basket from Holly's hand. Then, to their horror, she walked calmly across the shop and joined the queue, right behind the man.

'What does she think she's playing at?' Holly hissed. 'They'll see her!'

'It doesn't matter,' Josh whispered. 'The man doesn't know her. Even if Samantha does notice her, everybody in our school comes here – look, there are four more over there. And if she hears them talking it could help a lot!'

'Well, yes,' Holly nodded. 'I suppose so. Samantha might not see Amy anyway. Kennedy's jacket is so wide it would hide an elephant, never mind Amy.' She peeped round the stand again.

Josh hauled her back. 'Stop that!' he hissed. 'If they see people peering at them, that really will upset them! Come on – we'll go out before them, and watch to see which way they go when they leave. And don't look at Amy as we go.'

They walked out of the shop, trying not to look too innocent.

In the shop Samantha Gillingham was pretending not to know Mr Kennedy, not turning round to face him as she spoke. He wasn't looking at her, but staring round the shop. His face was unworried, but Amy knew he was checking that nobody was watching.

There was a woman at the front of the queue making a fuss because the plastic wrapping of a huge pink teddy bear was slightly split. The manager was called, and the whole queue was held up. It gave the kidnappers longer to talk, and the woman's loud voice gave them cover for their conversation. It even made them raise their own voices a little.

Amy tucked in behind Kennedy, as close as she could reasonably get, hoping that Samantha wouldn't look beyond him if she turned round. She could make out a few words here and there. 'OK – no sign of them . . . safe and sound down the hole …'

Amy started fishing in her pocket; did she have enough money for the Sellotape and balloons? She bent sideways to reach down to the bottom of her skirt pocket, and suddenly stiffened. There was a mirror behind the shelves on the wall opposite the queue. Because she was bent down slightly, she just caught a flickering reflection in the mirror. The kidnappers had moved close together, quite casually, but low down at arm's length, something, something small and white and square, like an envelope, was passed back from Samantha to her friend. As he eased away from Samantha, Amy saw Kennedy stow whatever it was away in an inner pocket of his big jacket.

He looked round carefully before he spoke again, but Amy was rummaging in her pockets, and his eyes passed right over her. 'Ta,' he muttered. 'Be sweating by now, eh? I'll get it to them tonight. No sense me hanging about too.' His voice changed for the last three words, as if they meant something special, and he gave a nasty chuckle.

Behind him. Amy was straining to catch every word, without being noticed. *"It"* must be the ransom demand. *"Sweating by now"* – that would be the Ogilvies, the kidnapped girl's parents, worrying about their daughter. Rotten pig! She strained her ears.

Samantha said something about a car. The man laughed. 'Yeah. Right off the track, see. Good idea, eh?' The queue moved forward. 'Ten more days, eh? And then Rio for me!'

Amy kept her head down, but Samantha paid for her tights and left without a backward glance.

Holly and Josh stood looking into the window of a greengrocer's and watched as Samantha turned into a café a few doors down. 'Drat it!' Holly hissed. 'She'll be there for ages, probably, and we've got to get back to school.'

Mr Kennedy bought his sweets and left, turning the other way. They started after him, but his van was parked just down the street, and he got in and drove off quickly. 'Drat it again!' Josh commented, before Holly could.

As Amy came out of the shop, her friends beckoned her over to join them, out of sight of the café. 'Well?' Holly demanded. 'What did you hear? I nearly died when you waltzed off like that!'

'Greatest coup of the century!' Amy boasted.

'Rio?' said Josh, when she had told them what she'd heard. 'He's going to Rio. Wow!'

'Not bad, eh?' demanded Amy. 'How about we try it? You two can kidnap me and demand a ransom!'

'Don't be silly, your mum and dad would pay us to keep you!' Josh retorted.

'At least it sounds as if she's still all right,' Amy said, sticking her tongue out at him. ' "Safe and sound down the hole," Samantha said.'

'And the envelope, or whatever it was — that would be proof they had her; a photograph of her holding today's papers, something like that,' said Josh.

'Lucy's hair, maybe,' Amy suggested. 'That dark red — it's unusual.'

'The "hole" must be inside the house. You said the Inspector put men on to watch the house right away, so she must still be there.' Holly was fretting.

'Yes. Or they'd have left already,' Josh agreed.

'And now they've been searched and Lucy hasn't been found, they must be feeling a bit safer.'

Amy was frowning. 'There was something else,' she muttered to herself. 'That "hanging about" – that wasn't a normal comment. Oh, well.' She shrugged. 'We'll find out!'

'We've got to find out!' Holly said. 'I can't stand thinking about that poor girl! But the police still won't believe us. They'd probably think we were just making it up.'

'Come on, or we'll be late back, and that won't help.' Josh urged them along the pavement towards the school. He was thinking hard. 'Somebody's got to get into the house, that's all. To have a look round. And more thoroughly than the police!'

'That won't be easy,' said Amy. 'The police went through it top to bottom, and I don't see Inspector Ross missing much.'

'No,' Holly agreed. 'We need to do it differently. At least it's Saturday tomorrow, so we'll have time. But how could we possibly do it?'

'The Inspector said there were burglar alarms – and anyway, one known burglar among us is more than enough!' joked Josh.

'Oh, shut up!' Amy frowned fiercely at him.

'Can we trick them somehow?' asked Holly. 'Maybe we could disguise ourselves as something different. So that they let us in themselves.'

'It would have to be one of you two. They know me,' Amy grumbled.

'Market researchers?' Holly suggested. 'No, they'd just shut the door.'

'Could we pretend to be workmen – plumbers, or something?' wondered Amy.

'We don't look old enough – and I *don't* look like a plumber,' Holly objected.

'That's what a disguise is for!' said Amy. 'Don't be defeatist! They let that glazier in. Maybe we could break some more of their windows?'

'Don't be silly!' Holly was quite alarmed. 'We can't do anything like that!'

'And what if we're wrong?' Josh asked.

Amy glowered at him. 'Whose side are you on?'

'We can't do anything that'll damage things, or hurt people,' Holly told her. 'We're in enough trouble. You especially. They'd never let you off a third time. So no fireworks to imitate gas explosions, or anything like that.'

'Oh, I suppose not,' Amy sighed. 'What about

stink bombs? To make them call in plumbers to check their drains?'

'You're hooked on plumbers!' Josh shook his head. 'It has to be something that they won't suspect, something absolutely ordinary.'

He swiped at a wasp circling round his head. 'Oh, drat these things, they're everywhere! I loathe wasps.'

'Don't do that!' Amy told him. 'If you scare it and it stings me I'll thump you! There was one on my arm while I was watching the house, licking at where the choc-ice had left a bit of sugar, I suppose. I didn't bother it, and it didn't bother me. There must be a nest up there somewhere. Hey – how do you write an essay on wasps?'

'With a very small pen,' said Josh. She stuck out her tongue at him again.

They suddenly realised Holly wasn't beside them. She was standing ten steps behind, in the middle of the pavement, with her mouth open.

'Hey, Holly!' Amy called. 'Wake up!'

'What is it?' Josh asked. 'Had an idea?'

'A whiz-banger of an idea!' Holly gasped, hurrying to catch up with them. 'A real super-duper gigantic colossal Sale of the Century genius-sized idea! Biological warfare!'

'What do you mean?' demanded Amy.

'*Wasps*! We'll use wasps!'

They gaped. 'You mean throw wasp nests into their garden?' Amy said blankly.

'Not me! No way!' Josh yelped, stopped dead in horror and had to be yanked out of the path of a pram. 'You're crazy!' he protested.

'What's crazy about it?' Amy demanded. 'I like it!'

'That's not a good sign!' Josh snapped. 'Don't be silly! You can't use wasps' nests like hand-grenades!'

'Why not? Think of the effect they'd have!' Amy exclaimed.

'No, no! I'm not that stupid!' Holly waved her hands at them. 'If we put sugar round there − lots and lots of sugar − every wasp in London would arrive, millions of them!'

'Zillions of them!' Amy made a horrible face. 'So?'

'So somebody would call the pest controllers, and they'd need to get into all the houses, to look for nests in sheds and attics and so on.'

'So?' Josh repeated.

'So why can't you get one of those paper boiler

suits, and pretend to be a pest controller? They all wear masks, so you could get away with it!'

'*Me?*' Josh almost squeaked it. 'I hate wasps! Why does it have to be me?'

'Because they know Amy, and I had the idea, so it's only fair,' said Holly. 'Everybody does something!'

They considered the idea in silence for a minute.

Amy's face spread into one huge grin. 'Oh, you beauty!' she yelled in glee, as she grabbed a startled Holly in her arms and began to whirl her round.

'Oh, stop that!' Holly snapped, going scarlet and tugging free. Amy could be really embarrassing. 'Get back to the point!' she said, pulling her school blouse straight. 'We can call the pest people ourselves – lots of firms, so that none of them'll realise Josh isn't with one of the others.'

'But won't people get stung?' Josh looked worried. 'Won't *I* get stung?'

'Not if you don't flap at the wasps. Everybody's so used to them by now, it's only idiots like you that try to hit them,' Holly said confidently. 'Besides, the pest control men will be getting rid of them. We'll be doing people a favour!'

'Thanks a bunch!' retorted Josh, desperate to find a way out. His face cleared. 'But if we scatter sugar, they'll see the crystals.'

'Yes, you're right,' said Amy.

'Sorry, Holly!' said Josh triumphantly. 'It wouldn't work.'

Holly bit her lip. She hadn't got that far.

'Syrup might be better,' Amy suggested, as they turned in at the school gate. 'Smear it about, on gates and so on – leaves, walls, out of sight.'

'But how?' Holly wondered. 'It can't be anywhere people would touch the stickiness and notice it, or it'd give the game away.'

Josh resigned himself to the idea, and started thinking hard. There didn't seem to be any way out, so at least they should plan it so that it wouldn't fail. 'What about a spray? Holly, your mum has a garden spray, doesn't she? If we dissolved sugar in water, couldn't we spray it about? Nobody would see it when it dried. But the wasps would still smell it.'

'Good thinking!' Amy cheered him. 'As long as it doesn't rain!'

'We'll just have to hope for the best!' Josh grinned back. He almost hoped it would pour! Then his shoulders slumped. 'But when? When can we do it? We'd need to do it in the dark, but we can't get out late.'

'Aha! My turn for an idea!' Amy declared in triumph. 'Did anybody's parents say anything about staying in bed in the morning? My mum's always trying to get me up early, so let's get up *really* early, while they're all still asleep! Say, four o'clock?'

'Four? You did say four o'clock? In the morning? Amy, that's your worst joke ever!' Josh liked his sleep.

'Not four, please, Amy!' begged Holly.

Amy shrugged. 'OK – five. It'll be dark till after six. That should give us plenty of time to do it, and still get home before anybody knows we've been out. And yes, you can get up that early, Josh, so stop making those faces!'

Some of Holly's class-mates came up at that moment and interrupted them. 'Hey, Holly! Show us the balloon trick!'

'Bet she can't,' one said.

'How much?' Amy demanded.

The girl stared. 'How much what?'

'How much do you bet? I've got–' Amy

remembered she'd spent all her money on the balloons. But Holly would give it back to her. 'Er – I've got about two pounds. Bet you fifty pence she can do it?'

The other older girls were laughing now, seeing their friend's bluff called. 'OK, Emily? Fifty pence? Go on!' they urged.

'No!' Emily declared roughly. 'I won't bet you fifty pence. You've got two pounds – OK, I'll bet you the lot! Two pounds says she can't do it!'

Amy gulped slightly, but she couldn't back down. 'OK,' she said. 'You're on!'

Holly was looking peeved. 'This is a bad idea,' she declared.

'It isn't gambling,' Amy announced happily. 'It's a sure thing!'

'I certainly hope so!' Holly said. 'It's just that I've never actually done this trick. I've only read about it in Jamie's book.'

Amy stared. 'You mean you haven't tried it out?' In her surprise, her voice rose so that they could all hear her.

Holly shook her head.

'Oh, great!' Amy moaned.

Everybody laughed, Emily loudest of all.

Holly opened the packet, blew up a big green balloon and tied a knot in the end.

'Ladies and gentlemen,' Amy announced at the top of her voice to their friends as they gathered round, 'the Great Holliberri will now amaze you with her astonishing magical feats! And hands! Lo and behold how the unbreakable laws of – er – balloonautics and elastixicity are broken before your very eyes! Hocus – pocus – diplodocus!' She waved a hand toward Holly.

Holly just stood and looked at her. 'Are you quite finished?' she asked sarcastically. 'Can I start now? You're sure? Thank you!'

Amy put her thumb to her nose and wiggled her fingers at Holly.

Laughing, Holly tore off a bit of Sellotape about four centimetres long, and stuck it down on to the end of the balloon. Then she got out a safety pin, poised it above the middle of the strip of Sellotape, and pressed down. Everybody – especially Amy – watched eagerly.

The pin made a dent, and suddenly went in – and the balloon didn't burst!

Holly drew the pin out again, slowly. With a hiss of escaping air the balloon started to collapse. Everyone cheered.

'Magic!' Amy shouted, grinning in relief. 'So hand over the money, Emily!'

The bigger girl looked as if she was going to refuse, but everybody was watching her. Reluctantly, she reached into her pocket and hunted out two pound coins. 'There you are!' she grunted as she handed them over. 'Bet it wouldn't work again!'

Amy's face lit up. 'How much? I've got four pounds now!'

'Oh give over!' Emily snarled and turned away. Amy grinned cockily.

'Show us again, Holly!' someone said. Holly shrugged and tried again.

This time, the balloon burst.

Everybody roared at the expression on Emily's face. And on Amy's.

The bell rang. 'See you,' said Josh. 'Five o'clock tomorrow!'

'I'll get the sugar and Mum's spray,' said Holly, 'and meet you both at our corner.'

'OK. We'd better check our bike lights tonight,' Josh suggested.

Amy stared at him. 'I can't. My parents would be so astonished, they'd think I was ill!'

Holly poked her. 'Just remember – this early start

business is your idea, Amy! If you sleep in, and we get up, we'll never forgive you!'

'Hoi!' Amy shouted back as they split up. 'Hoi, Holly! What about the money for the balloons?'

'I'll need it for the sugar! You be satisfied with your winnings!' Holly called back, waved, then turned towards her classroom.

6

Let us Spray!

Holly took a few minutes that evening to slip out to the garden shed and check whether her idea would work. Making sure nobody was watching, she took a pinch of sugar from the bowl, mixed it with some water, and sprinkled it on the shed door. After only a minute, a couple of wasps stopped to investigate, and seemed very happy with the result. When they flew off, Holly quickly washed off the rest of the sugar before the shed filled with wasps!

The garden spray had a tank that held about five litres, with a handle on top that pulled up and down to pump up the pressure inside, and a long thin plastic tube with a nozzle at the end. When you pressed the lever on the nozzle, the liquid shot out. You could adjust it to either a fine, wide spray, which didn't go very far, or a long squirt like a fountain jet. She made sure it was working, and left it ready just inside the shed door.

Holly went to bed early, at nine o'clock, saying she was very tired. She set her alarm for four-thirty, and stuck it under her pillow; she didn't want to wake her parents, or Jamie! However, she was so excited that she woke up even before the alarm sounded. She got up quietly, pulled on an old sweat-shirt and jeans and her darkest jacket, and sneaked downstairs.

The four kilogram bags of sugar she had bought on her way home from school were still in her saddle-bags. Holly strapped the spray tank on the carrier of her bike, and cycled to the corner of the road.

It was cold and dark. She hoped the others had remembered!

A faint light wobbled round the corner, and Amy used her feet to stop beside her. 'Hi!' she whispered. 'I made it! Can't put my brakes on, they squeak. They'd wake everybody. And my lights battery's just about flat – I should have checked like Josh said!'

She rubbed her hands to warm them. 'Brr! Freezing, isn't it? Oh, I brought a bucket for mixing.'

'Fine, I didn't think of that! But what'll we do for water?' Holly whispered. 'Will we have to carry it from here?'

'Don't worry,' Amy reassured her. 'There's a tap behind the house that's for sale. It was damp underneath, so it must have been dripping. I guess it hasn't been turned off.'

'That's OK, then.' Holly yawned. 'That's funny! I'd have thought the excitement would keep me awake, but I'm still yawning.'

Amy fished in her pocket. 'Look, chocolate for emergency rations. Want a bit? I've only had one bite off it. No? Oh, well, suit yourself.' She took a big chunk. 'Look, there's Josh!'

Josh had a games bag with him. 'Hi!' he murmured, and yawned uncontrollably. 'This had better work, Holly!'

'It will!' Holly assured him. 'I tried it!'

'It's got to!' Amy whispered. 'She's got her fingers, toes and eyes crossed!'

Josh shivered. 'I brought three flasks of boiling water, to help dissolve the sugar.'

'Let's go,' said Holly quietly. 'And let's hope we don't meet any police cars on the way!'

They didn't. They got to the house safely, and hid their bikes round the corner where Amy had put hers before.

Below them, one of the windows of the kidnap house was lit.

'There's somebody up,' Josh murmured. 'Someone standing guard, or something. What do we do now?'

After watching for a minute, Amy shook her head. 'There's a blind on that window. It was like that before, remembered? And it was down all day yesterday too. I don't know – maybe there's nobody there, it's just to keep burglars away. Or—'

Holly took it up. 'Maybe that's where they're keeping Lucy Ogilvie. Nobody can see out, anyway, not while the blind's down. We've got to risk it.'

They exchanged glances, and all nodded.

'Right, how do we organise this?' asked Josh.

'I'll mix,' said Amy. 'Give me a flask, Josh. I'll put the sugar in the bucket first, then hot water, and when it's dissolved as far as it's going to, I'll fill it up from the tap. OK?'

'Right,' said Holly. 'And keep watch while we're spraying. If you see anybody moving—'

'I'll hoot like an owl!' Amy said enthusiastically.

'No! Your owls sound like ships' sirens! Just hiss. We'll be listening for it, and we'll freeze,' Holly told her.

Josh looked at her. 'You're tallest. You do the spraying,' he suggested. 'I'll carry the spray and keep it pumped up.'

'Fine,' Holly nodded.

There were difficulties they'd not thought of.

Even swirled about in Josh's boiling water, the sugar took ages to dissolve.

When they first turned on the tap, they jumped; the water sounded like a roll of drums as it poured into the big orange bucket! But nobody seemed to have heard, and Amy found that if she let it run on to her hand first, that cut the noise down a lot.

The spray, with its heavy body and long tube, was awkward to move, especially since it didn't have a carrying handle. It took a lot more pumping than Josh had expected to pressurise the tank, and if he wasn't careful it made a clacking noise.

But at last, they were ready with the first lot of sugar solution.

'OK!' said Holly, drawing a deep breath. 'Let's go!'

Amy grinned in the darkness. 'You mean, "Let us spray!" ' The others made faces at her, but it broke the tension and they all felt better.

They did the kidnap house first. If they didn't get that one done, they might as well forget the whole plan.

'You wait here until I take the tank down,' whispered Josh. 'If anybody comes out, I'll run – and if I have to leave the spray, at least they won't know what it's for! And it'll be less worrying for them if there's just one of me, rather than a gang.'

He climbed the fence, heaved the tank over after himself, and very, very cautiously lifted it down the steps through the three-foot-high terraces. Holding their breath, Amy and Holly watched for movement inside any of the windows as the tank bumped against Josh's legs and the long tube threatened to trip him, but he made it all right. At last, out of sight against the back wall of the house, Josh beckoned to Holly to creep down after him.

Then he kept the pressure up, while Holly reached up to squirt the sugary water over the walls. She tried to keep it off the windows, in case the film of sugar made a mark and was noticed. The jet reached the eaves easily, and the fine spray soaked the brickwork and the trees and bushes round about. It sounded a bit like rain.

Holly paid special attention to the caves above the window with the light, just above her head. If that really was where the girl was being held, that was where the K.I.D.Z. would want to have a look!

Amy watched for a minute, and then got on with mixing the next lot of sugar solution.

She stayed alert for any noise or movement on the road above her or the houses around, as well as in the kidnap house itself. A few early birds started chirping and twittering in the bushes round about. Some little animals rustled occasionally among the leaves, making her jump. *Rats*? She wondered. *Oh, yuck!* She shivered, and told herself that it was just because she was cold.

On the whole, it stayed peaceful. She only had to hiss twice.

The first time was for a police car driving along Orangery Crescent. Luckily, Josh and Holly were behind the house.

Amy had another chunk of chocolate, to cheer herself up.

The other time was a lucky mistake. Holly and Josh were spraying the bushes by the front drive of the kidnap house, carefully keeping off the crunchy gravel. They emptied the tank, lifted it to come back for a refill, and crept along the edge of the weed-filled flower border to the cement path that ran up beside the house.

Just then a little black-and-white terrier came rootling round the gardens and bins of the road above. It smelt Amy and came over to find out who was up so early. At the first sign of movement, Amy hissed, and below her Josh and Holly shrank in against the wall and froze.

When Amy saw it was a stray dog, she patted its wiry head and tried to shoo it away, but she couldn't make a noise, and it wouldn't go.

Then Holly dropped the spray nozzle with a clatter. Her heart nearly stopped. How could she have been so careless?

Almost at once, the back door opened. A man came out. Josh and Holly crouched motionless, pressed in against the side of the house, with no cover.

Above them, watching from behind the fence, Amy bit her fingers to stop herself from crying out. It was Mr Gillingham! He peered suspiciously round the dark garden. If he went to the corner of the house and looked round it, he couldn't help seeing her friends . . .

She took the last bit of chocolate from her pocket. The little dog sniffed it, and licked at it. She flipped the sweet down over the fence, to land on the terraces below. 'Go on, boy!' she breathed in the dog's floppy ear.

The terrier wriggled through a hole in the fence and started sniffing among the flowers and shrubs to find the chocolate, wagging his stumpy tail and whining with excitement.

Mr Gillingham stared up, saw the dog, and shouted at it quietly. 'Shoo! Clear out!' He waved his arms, and threw a stone at it. The terrier finally found the chocolate, picked it up and scrabbled back up through the fence and away on to the upper road.

Silence fell again. With a last look round the terraces, Mr Gillingham went back inside.

The three K.I.D.Z. sighed in relief. That was a closer call than they'd want ever again!

Amy shook her head. The sacrifices she made for her friends!

Each bucketful filled the sprayer about one and a half times. By the fourth bucket, they had treated the kidnap house and garden, the gardens on either side of it, the one they were in, and its neighbouring ones. They'd run out of hot water by now, and the sugar was taking even longer to dissolve. And the sky was turning grey, above the glow of the street-lights.

'That's the last of the sugar,' Amy said. 'Just this bucket, and that's us finished.'

'Too true!' Josh puffed, stretching. He rubbed his arms. 'Pumping that spray is easy when you start, but when you go on and on and on at it, it gets too much like hard work!'

'It's time we got off home anyway. It's nearly six,' Holly sighed. Her wrists and arms were cold and aching from holding out the dribbly spray for such a long time. 'We'll have paper-boys and milkmen round any minute,' she said. 'Come on, Josh, last time!'

They finished the spray off quickly with a long jet right across the garden directly up from kidnap house and into the garden on the other side. 'That should do it,' Josh said. 'I'm whacked!'

'This will be wasp paradise as soon as the sun hits it tomorrow,' Holly said, easing her stiff, sticky fingers.

'You mean today.' Josh yawned like a hippo.

Amy grinned at them, offensively bright and cheerful. 'Come on,' she said. 'I've packed everything up on to the bikes.'

Holly just had to strap the spray on to her carrier again, and then they free-wheeled wearily back off down Grove Road, only turning on their lights when they were well away.

They stopped together under the street-light at the end of Holly's road, to make plans. 'Right,' Amy said. 'What next?'

Holly yawned and stretched. 'Well, we'll meet here, about nine? That'll give the wasps time to find it all.'

'And give us another couple of hours to sleep,' Josh said. 'Boy, do I need it! 'Bye. See you then. Oh – Dad's got a blue nylon boiler suit he uses for working on the car. It's a bit too big for me, but I can roll up the arms and legs. I'll bring it along.' He yawned again, and pedalled off.

Holly yawned as well. 'I need to sleep, too,' she

sighed. 'I'm almost too sleepy to worry if it'll work or not.'

'Not me,' Amy chirped. 'I feel fine!' She was suddenly surprised by an enormous yawn too. They were both laughing as they cycled home.

7

Josh the Apprentice

At nine o'clock, Holly was waiting again at her gate for her friends to arrive. She felt surprisingly alert, considering the sleep she'd missed. She hoped the others would too.

This time Josh arrived first. 'You look dreadful, Josh!' Holly greeted him.

He made a face. 'If I look half as bad as I feel, I wouldn't beat Frankenstein's monster in a beauty contest! Dad caught me last night – this morning, I mean. When I got in.'

'Oh, Christmas!' Holly gasped. 'What did he say? What did *you* say?'

Josh shrugged. 'I've got till twelve noon to tell him all about it. He's being great about it, I think.

But I don't know what he'll be like if I can't give him a good explanation at twelve. This plan had better work, Holly. I can't let him down!'

She nodded. 'I know what you mean. But you won't! Even if it doesn't work, it can't do any harm.' She jumped at a screech of bike brakes behind her, but didn't turn round. 'Hi, Amy.'

'How did you know it was me?' Amy demanded.

'Who else's bike makes such a racket?' Holly shook her head sadly. 'Have you never heard of oil? Spies are supposed to move silently!'

'Oh, I'll do it some day,' Amy grinned chirpily. 'Are you ready? Come on, then!'

'Hang on a minute,' Josh said. 'Let's get organised. Have you got anything for phone calls?'

Amy's face beamed. 'Yep! A phone card.'

Holly added, 'And I've got the numbers of all the local pest control firms out of the Yellow Pages. There's a phone box not far from the end of Orangery Crescent.'

'Right,' said Josh. 'But we'd better go up there first, and see what's happening.'

Holly nodded. 'Yeah, we'd really look like idiots, calling up wasp killers if there weren't any wasps!'

When they cycled up the hill, they found a van already there on the upper road, with "POTTS & CO, PEST CONTROL" on the side. Another van was parking down on Orangery Crescent.

'Great!' Amy said, her eyes gleaming. 'I never thought it'd go *this* well!'

'Are you surprised?' Holly asked. 'Look at the place!'

Every surface in the gardens around had a faint sheen. Not enough to be noticed, unless you looked for it specially, but the sugar was there. And it was certainly attracting wasps.

They stared round. 'Wowee,' Amy whispered. 'It looks like every leaf's got a wasp on it, and three more circling to land!'

Josh shuddered. 'I didn't imagine – I never thought it'd be like this!'

Holly looked at him in some dismay. 'What's wrong, Josh?'

Amy grinned. 'He doesn't like wasps! Don't worry, Josh, they're not going to pick you up and carry you off to their nests!'

Josh swallowed. 'I don't just not like wasps, Amy. I hate them! They make my skin crawl! And I've never seen as many as this before!'

'Do you think you'll be all right?' asked Holly. Josh was almost as white as a sheet. If she'd known, she'd never have suggested this.

'Oh, yes.' Josh gulped, clenching his jaw. He'd have to be!

'Should I go and phone some more firms?' Amy asked.

'No,' Holly said. 'I will. I sound older than you. That van's from Potts & Co.'

Josh peered round the end of the garage. 'That's Pestaway down there.'

'Right.' Holly ticked them off on her list. 'I don't need to call them. You get into your boiler suit, while I phone.'

'I'll watch your back, Josh,' Amy offered, 'to see you don't get any wasps inside the suit!'

Josh's stomach heaved. He gritted his teeth. 'Don't say things like that! Don't even think them!'

From the phone box on the corner, Holly called up the first of her numbers. When a man answered, she took a deep breath, and started to gabble in a grown-up voice. 'Hello? Is that Free 'n' Ezi pest controllers? Hello? Hello? Oh, thank goodness! We need you right away! I don't know what's happened, but it's dreadful, the wasps this morning, they're swarming everywhere – I don't know what to do – I can't breathe! You've got to come! Please!'

The man she was speaking to was trying to interrupt, stop her, calm her down. 'Yes, madam! What's wrong – wasps, you say? What's your name? Where are you speaking from?'

'Orangery Crescent!' Holly squawked. She suddenly realised she didn't know the number of the kidnap house. 'It's an emergency! Come right away!'

To her relief, the man said. 'Don't worry, madam, we've already had a call from that road, and one of our vans is on its way.'

'Oh, good! Oh, terribly good!' Holly rang off, cutting off his request for her name.

She did the same thing twice more. The second firm had also been called in already, but the third asked for a name and address before agreeing to come out. Holly made them up – 'Mrs Anderson, 19 Grove Road!'

The girl in the office said, 'Thank you. The cost will be £60 for the first two hours, and £20 for each hour needed after that. Is that satisfactory?'

'Yes – oh, yes! Come quickly!' Holly exclaimed,

and rang off. *Oh, dear!* she thought. *If each of these firms is charging that, the K.I.D.Z. have cost a lot of people a lot of money today! We didn't think of that!*

Then she grinned to herself. *We can pay them back out of the reward*!

By the time she got back to her friends, wincing away from the wasps that bombed round her like bullets, three more vans had already arrived, two in Grove Road, one in Orangery Crescent. One woman she passed was saying;'No, I didn't call you, but I'm delighted you're here. It's an invasion!'

The pest control men were already spreading out through the gardens, spraying as they went. The sharp sting of the chemicals caught at Holly's throat, and Josh was coughing.

'Come on,' Amy encouraged him. 'Just be glad you're not a wasp. It's not that bad!'

'Oh, no?' he wheezed. 'Look, all the men have masks on!'

'Well, go and ask if they'll give you one too!' Holly said. 'That'll make you look even more like one of them.'

Amy nodded. 'Yes, go on. They can only say no!'

Josh looked doubtful, but went out to Grove Road.

A shortish, fattish man in blue overalls was standing by the nearest van door mixing chemicals from a huge drum, in a big spray tank.

Just as Josh reached the van, the man finished and screwed the cap on the tank tightly. He grinned at Josh, waved round at the swarms of insects, and shook his head admiringly. 'You've got a right dose here, haven't you, son? Where'd they all come from, eh? I've never seen anything like this before.'

'I don't know,' Josh said. 'But there's millions round a house just down the hill there.'

'Oh, yeah?' the man said. 'Special, is it? Let's have a squint.' He carefully clipped the top down on the drum, and rolled off down the path of the house where the van was parked, directly above the kidnap house.

Josh followed him and pointed. 'Down there. See?' Round the eaves of the kidnap house, where Holly had sprayed especially vigorously, the air was thick with insects.

'A real big nest that is, son!' the man nodded. He looked round. Men were working in two gardens already, but none in the garden of the kidnap house. The man grinned. 'Ta, son. We get in first, we get paid for it.'

He was turning away when Josh had a great idea. 'Can I come in with you and watch?' he asked. 'Give you a hand, maybe?'

'Why not?' the man agreed, giving a big shrug. 'Could do with an extra pair of hands.'

He eyed Josh's blue overalls, the sleeves and legs rolled up half a dozen times, and grinned. 'Well, you're dressed for it, but you need a mask, with all this gunk in the air. It won't do your lungs any good, eh? Here you are.' He handed over a plastic mask and a gauze filter, with an elastic band to go round Josh's head to hold it on.

'Thanks, sir!' Josh said. He hadn't even had to ask!

'No problem,' the man grinned. 'Haven't you ever put one on before? This way, son.' He fitted the gauze pad into its holder and popped it over Josh's mouth and nose. 'Pull the strap at the side till it's tight, OK? That's it. But you can let the mask down round your neck for now, son. We haven't got going yet, not properly.'

He looked Josh over, and shook his head. 'Here's a cap you can have, it'll keep them out of your ears, eh?' He handed over an old baseball cap.

Josh was glad to tug it down over his hair. With the cap and the mask, he felt like a train robber.

'Do as you're told, mind!' the man warned him, climbing into his van. 'Dangerous stuff this is! No mucking about!'

'No, of course not!' Josh assured him. This was better than he'd hoped for! He gave a triumphant thumbs-up sign to where he knew the girls were watching and swung up into the seat next to the driver. *Could it be better?* he thought. *Arriving right in the pest control van! Magic!*

'Er – I'm Josh,' he said.

The driver reached over to shake hands while swinging round the corner. 'Archie Potts. Good to meet you, Josh! Looking for a Saturday job?'

'Well – maybe,' Josh said nervously.

'Steady work, this is, in the summer. Not so hot in winter – not so hot in winter, eh?' Archie rolled with laughter at his own joke as they turned into Orangery Crescent.

'I – er – I don't like wasps,' Josh told him.

To his surprise, Archie just laughed even louder. 'Who does, son? Nasty vicious little beggars. That's what this job's all about! This is the house, eh?' He stopped the van and led Josh up the drive to ring the doorbell. 'But the average wasp, he's not interested in you—'

The door opened. A man stood there – the heavy-set man Josh had seen on the night of the raid. 'What is it? What's wrong?'

'What's wrong?' Archie snorted. 'Huh! Can't you see it? You got wasps, mate. You and the whole street, looks like!'

A girl appeared in the dark of the hall. 'Wasps?' she asked. 'Yeah, they're bad, Jim.'

Josh almost jumped for joy. This was Samantha Gillingham, but she'd called the man "Jim" although the Inspector had said Mr Gillingham's name was Arnold! One of them must be a false name – and as she hadn't called him "Dad" or something like that, he probably wasn't her father either!

The girl was nodding. 'It's real enough.'

'Yes, I know,' the man said. 'I'm allergic to wasps. I've been wishing we could get them seen to for days.'

'Well, here's us!' Archie beamed at them. He certainly didn't look like a policeman, and Josh could see the man relaxing slightly. 'Me and my apprentice here, we'll see them off for you! You got a nest right in your roof. Dunno how you didn't see them before. But we'll clear them off in a jiff. I'll give you a special price. We'll check right round your garden and attic. What do you say?'

Mr Gillingham was frowning suspiciously again, but the young woman tugged him aside. Josh just heard her whisper. 'It's OK, Jim! Down the hole, and lock the door – they can't . . . Odd if we don't. I mean—' she pointed to the haze of insects outside, and the two vans in the road – 'everybody else is. Fit in, you said!'

After a moment, Mr Gillingham nodded. However, he insisted on going out to check on the reported wasps' nest. The cloud of insects round the eaves instantly convinced him. He shuddered. 'I can't stand them!' he said. 'Right. Go ahead.'

Josh hid a grin. It had worked!

Archie beamed. 'We'll be with you in ten minutes. My mate Bobo's got the spray just now. He's the brawn, I'm the brains!' He gestured with his thumb to where a man in a blue boiler suit just like Josh's, but with a wide hat and veil to keep the wasps off his face, was spraying the garden above. The sight, and the lack of urgency, seemed to calm Mr Gillingham's nerves a bit.

'Yeah. Me and Josh here, we'll just have a squint round your garden, to see how many nests we can find, eh?' said Archie. 'Then we'll do them first, before we get stuck into the biggie up there.'

He pointed to the right. 'You take that side, Josh, and I'll go up here,' he said. 'Look up through the trees, right up in them. You're looking for roundish balls, hanging from branches. Greyish. Any size, see, from eggs to – oh, football, beach ball, OK?'

'OK, Archie,' Josh said, gulping slightly. The thought of actually finding a wasps' nest made him feel sick, but he couldn't run away. If he was pretending to be a wasp exterminator, well, he'd just have to act like one! He walked along the path, gritted his teeth and ducked in among the branches of the first tree.

Mr Gillingham stood at the back door of his house and watched.

OK, Josh thought. *Look up.* He shoved some branches aside to get in near the trunk, and tilted his head back. Then he froze.

Twenty centimetres above his nose was a round ball of rough grey paper.

It was bigger than his head. Much bigger.

It had a small hole at the bottom, and wasps were crawling in and out. Dozens of them.

Josh's spine turned to ice. He could feel his lips and eyebrows trying to crawl away and tuck themselves out of danger behind his ears.

He stiffened his knees enough to walk, backed out quietly, and had to try three times before he could control his voice enough to call, 'Archie! I've found one.'

Mr Gillingham came nervously over, too. As he and Archie peered through the branches, Josh was quite pleased to see that Mr Gillingham looked as scared as he had been himself.

'Well done, son!' Archie slapped Josh on the back. 'Good start, eh?'

'Dear heavens!' Mr Gillingham exclaimed. 'Get rid of it!' His voice was high and almost hysterical. 'I never guessed – so close – get it out of here!'

'OK, OK,' Archie reassured him. 'Soon as Bobo finishes up there.'

Mr Gillingham stared at him and ran to the house.

Josh had to nerve himself to move up to the next tree. Archie gave him a thumbs-up sign. Josh returned it, gulped, and pulled his mask up. It wasn't as good as a full veil, but it was better than nothing! He pushed the next lot of branches aside.

He nearly jumped out of his skin as a voice just by his feet hissed, '*Psst*!'

'Don't do that!' he hissed back.

'How's it going?' Amy whispered. She was crouching under a bush in the next garden with a handkerchief over her mouth as a kind of mask. The spray was starting to drift over.

'OK. I've got a job! I've just found a huge nest in the next tree down!' Josh told her. 'I'll be in the house in a few minutes!'

'Talk about lucky!' she grinned. 'What's the wasp man like?'

'Archie? He's great,' said Josh. 'He likes the same kind of bad jokes you do!'

Amy dropped the hankie enough to stick her tongue out at him, grinning.

Josh glanced round. 'Look, I've got to go. There's Mr Gillingham coming out – no, he's driving off. That's just Samantha left in the house, I think. That should make it easier to look round. Wish me luck!'

8

The Hole

Archie and Josh found another nest among the bushes. Josh just wished he could get used to the wasps!

'Come on, son,' Archie said. 'We'll go and check indoors, OK?'

Right, Josh thought. *Now for it! A hole, and a locked door, Samantha said. In the cellar, maybe? But it means an open door isn't worth checking. That'll cut it down a lot!*

Archie rolled over to the back door, knocked and barged in. Samantha Gillingham was doing a crossword, having a cup of coffee and a biscuit. She stared at him, and said sarcastically, 'Do come in!'

'Got to get up to your attic now,' Archie

announced. He eyed the coffee and biscuits. 'Smells good, that does!'

She didn't take him up on it. She just stood up decisively and led them out to the hall. 'I'll come with you. Have you got a torch?'

'Er—' Josh hesitated, but Archie heard him.

'What is it, Josh?'

'Maybe there's something in the cellar. Can I look?'

He had expected Samantha to refuse to let him go off on his own, but she didn't seem worried. 'Sure,' she said calmly, pointing to the door. 'Down there. I don't think there's anything there, but you never know.' She chuckled smugly. 'Mind the steps, they're steep. Somebody fell down yesterday.' She started up the stairs, followed by Archie.

The cellar floor was solid concrete. It had been scratched in all the corners, and all the old furniture lying about in it had just been moved. That must have been the police, Josh figured. There were no locked doors, no holes. Besides, Samantha hadn't been nervous about Josh coming down here. No, he decided; there was nothing here.

Archie and Samantha were upstairs out of sight. Josh checked quickly round the ground floor. He found a dining-room; a room with lots of empty bookshelves; the kitchen; a utility room; a nursery with Peter Rabbit wallpaper; and in the centre, a small, windowless cubby-hole with deep shelves right up to the ceiling all round – an old-fashioned butler's pantry. Only the kitchen and dining-room had any furniture.

Again, there were no holes or locked doors.

Josh tip-toed up to the landing. Open doors showed the living-room where the girl had broken the window, a bedroom and three empty rooms. Two other doors were shut.

Samantha was standing on the loft ladder that led up through a trapdoor, her top half through into the attic. 'Can't you see anything?' she demanded.

'Not a sausage!' Archie's voice rumbled beyond her. 'You got too many corners, pet. There could be a dozen nests in here, hid in the shadows.'

She puffed in annoyance. 'Give me the torch!' she snapped, and climbed right up into the loft.

One of the shut doors led to a small bedroom. There was nothing there.

Josh turned to the last door. It was locked.

Suddenly he was breathless. This – he looked round to work it out in his head, and nodded – this was the room where the light was on all night, and the blind drawn.

It was the kind of lock that just pulls shut, not one where you have to turn the key to lock it. *That girl must have the key safe*, he thought. *I'll never get in*.

He glared round. There must be some way in, surely?

Hang on! Above the lintel over the door, a tiny gleam of light flashed on the ceiling. He took a step up the loft ladder to see; yes, there was something there, tucked away on top of the door-frame, that for an instant had reflected the torch shining from the loft trapdoor.

It was a key!

It must be completely hidden, except when there was a light being flashed around the attic; like now, this one time, because of Holly's wasp idea.

Josh could just reach the key, stretching on tip-toe. He snatched it up and fitted it into the lock without another thought. There was no time to waste.

To his surprise, he had to turn the key twice. It was a deadlock as well as a spring catch, to give double security for the kidnappers.

Now, though, the door opened a fraction. Success!

He tucked the key back on its ledge.

He drew a deep breath, pushed the door half open, slid in and shut the door behind him. He could still get out; the handle was on his side.

His heart sank in pure disappointment.

It was another bedroom. The blind was still drawn, above an unmade bed. A small chest of drawers and a biggish built-in wardrobe with a central sliding slatted door filled the wall opposite. The wardrobe door was half open. Clothes were hanging in the left-hand end, and shoes and some big cases lay on the floor. There was nothing else, no girl lying drugged on the bed, no gaping secret passage; nothing.

So, he wondered, *why was it locked with this fancy lock?*

Suddenly he heard Samantha demand, 'Where's that boy got to?'

Archie's voice rumbled, 'Maybe he went back out. Don't worry, pet, he'll be about!'

If she's really a kidnapper, she'll worry! Josh thought. He could hear Samantha coming down the loft ladder, and there was a little grunt outside the door. She was stretching up for the key!

Josh looked round in horror. He mustn't be found! But where could he hide?

Under the bed? No, that was the first place she'd look.

There were no curtains to hide behind.

There was only one place – the wardrobe. He dived into it.

The door lock rattled as the girl tried to turn the key twice and it jammed. She swore.

That second gave Josh just enough time.

He stepped over the cases and shoes right to the end of the wardrobe where the clothes hung behind the solid bit of front that the door slid behind, and knelt on the floor under a coat, his head down on his knees.

Samantha charged into the room. He heard the bed being shifted, and then the sliding door of the wardrobe was slammed fully back. It caught his hair and jammed it against the end wall, but he couldn't cry out.

Samantha stuck her head into the wardrobe.

She peered into the dark end where Josh crouched, and reached in to shake the clothes and push right through to the wall, to check there was no-one standing there.

She didn't look down.

Crouched in the dark, Josh felt that his back must be obvious, sticking up like a camel's hump . . . but Samantha didn't look down.

Then she turned to the other end. She stood a case on end and leaned forward, reached down and tugged at something heavy. Josh didn't dare turn his head to see what she was doing. She grunted as she pulled something up, and Josh heard a thud. There was a strangled moan.

'Shut up, you!' Samantha's voice was a snarl. 'Keep quiet! Or I'll flip your lid down for good, and forget about you!'

There was silence. Josh scarcely dared breathe.

Samantha huffed in satisfaction. 'That's it! That's better! That's a good little rich girl! You be dead quiet, right? Or dead! Your choice!'

She bumped the heavy thing again, and shoved herself back up out of the wardrobe. The door slid over. Josh could hear her, in the bedroom, just inches from his head, muttering. 'Where the devil's that boy gone?'

There was a metallic click.

Josh's heart lurched. Just two nights before on *Spyglass,* the K.I.D.Z.'s favourite television programme, the villain had cocked a pistol. The click had sounded just like that.

Then the door opened and shut, and the key turned.

That was a close call! Josh thought.

He eased his back and lifted a hand to rub his head. The door slamming past him had actually torn out some of his hair! He left the door shut for a moment. Enough light came in through the gaps between the slats for him to see what he was doing, and he didn't want to risk being caught outside in the bedroom, especially not if Samantha had a gun.

Josh crawled over the big cases, along to the other end of the wardrobe, to where there was a clear space on the floor. He felt all over it, but it was quite smooth. But as he turned round, he put his knee on the heel of a shoe that was lying there, and fell sideways, so that his hand landed right in the front corner of the wardrobe floor – and the floor shifted underneath him.

He tried again; yes, when he pressed down hard, right against the wall, the floor he was kneeling on lifted, just a fraction. He'd have to open the wardrobe door and get out before he could do it properly.

Oh, well, Josh told himself, *I can't stop now*!

He opened the door and listened; there was no noise. He crawled out, turned and reached back inside. It was very awkward to get any pressure into that corner, but when he pressed down as hard as he could an irregular patch of floor about sixty centimetres across tilted slightly. He could just get the fingers of his left hand in under the edge nearest him and lift it, using all his strength, to lean it gingerly against the wall. It was heavy and solid, with a thick felt padding underneath. When it was down, and the cases slid on top, who'd know it was there? It wouldn't even sound hollow.

And under it was a hole.

Where could it go? Down there, Josh thought. It was the butler's pantry. They must have taken out the shelves from one end, built a false wall, and replaced the shelves so that nobody could knock against the wall and hear that it was hollow. Nobody would notice the little bit cut out among the corners and alcoves of all the small rooms.

Josh peered down into the blackness.

He reached down towards a dark lump he could just make out at arm's length.

His hand touched hair. It was someone's head!

Outside, Amy was fretting. 'What's happening?' she whispered for the tenth time.

Holly shrugged. 'Will you stop asking that? How on earth should I know?' She choked at the stink of the spray drifting across the gardens.

'Watch out or they'll hear you. You cough like a cannon!' Amy warned her.

Holly rolled her eyes. 'Tough! What should I do? Just stop breathing?'

They were crouching together under the laurel bushes at the corner of the garden of the "For Sale" house, peering down through the fence and the trees.

'It's dead as a doornail!' Holly muttered.

'I wonder why we say doornails?' Amy whispered. 'Coffin nails would be far deader.'

'Shut up!' Holly snapped at her. 'Don't talk about coffins!'

Amy almost snapped back, but she realised that Holly was frightened for Josh, and nervous. 'OK,' she said quietly.

Holly glanced over at her. 'Sorry,' she said. 'It's just—'

'I know,' said Amy. 'It's the strain. This waiting, doing nothing is worse than anything.'

Holly nodded. 'I hope Josh's all right.'

Inside the house, Josh was finding it hard to breathe, too. The head twitched under his hand, and the frightened whimper came again.

'Hello!' he whispered. 'Don't be scared – I'm not one of them! I've come to help you. Are you Lucy Ogilvie?'

Under his hand, the head nodded once, then over and over again, rolling desperately, moaning and grunting below him.

'Shh!' he hissed. 'Keep quiet! Keep still or they'll find us!'

Almost at once, Lucy stopped heaving about, although Josh could hear her breathing fast and hard through her nose.

'Are you gagged?' Josh whispered. She nodded. 'And tied up?' Another nod.

Feeling round the hole, he found straps leading down into it, and other straps over the girl's shoulders, like a parachute harness. 'Are you – you can't be just hanging there?' He couldn't believe anybody would be so cruel – but it was true!

Lucy nodded and struggled for a second, but then she managed to stop, hanging quietly again.

'You're doing great!' Josh muttered to encourage her. He heaved with all his strength at the straps, but he couldn't lift her, or reach down to the release buckle.

'I can't move you! I can't get you out by myself. I'm sorry, but I'm going to have to go and get the police. They'll know what to do.'

But would they believe him? After two false alarms? How could he convince the Inspector? He must find something, and quickly, quickly. Samantha was looking for him!

Suddenly he had an idea. He reached down as far as he dared. He could feel Lucy's neck. Round it there was a necklace. 'Sorry about this!' He gave the chain of the necklace a sharp tug, and it came loose in his hands.

For good measure, he pulled out a few strands of her hair. 'Sorry!' Josh whispered again. 'But I have to prove it's you!'

He carefully tucked the necklace and the

distinctive red hairs away in the pocket of his shirt under his boiler suit, and zipped it up again. 'Look, I have to go!' he whispered. 'I'll be back as quick as I can. It won't be long – not now that I can tell them exactly where you are. I'm not deserting you! We'll be back soon, I promise!'

Lucy squawked through her gag, and started to struggle again. Josh felt sick that he had to leave her dangling helpless and terrified, but he just couldn't help her, not alone!

'Quick as I can! I promise!' he whispered. He lowered the trapdoor gently, closed the wardrobe behind him and headed for the door.

It was locked from outside, of course. So he couldn't get out that way.

Right. He'd have to go out the window.

Josh was just climbing on the bed when he heard a car draw up in the drive just below. Mr Gillingham and another man got out.

Samantha ran out to them from the back door, calling, 'There's a boy missing. And the bedroom door – it wasn't properly locked. Yes – *that* room! We've got to find him!'

Mr Gillingham didn't waste words. 'Bill, you stay here. Hunt round.' He reached inside the breast of his jacket and hurried with the girl towards the back door.

He has a gun too! Josh thought. His heart nearly stopped with fright.

What could he do?

9

A Chase

Get out! I've got to get out! It hammered in Josh's brain. Maybe Amy and Holly could help somehow; it was a faint chance, but all he had.

He pushed aside the blind, and reached up to shove up the bottom sash. Outside, the air and the wall were still thick with wasps.

Josh hadn't even time to think about being scared of them.

Holly and Amy had seen the car arrive, and the kidnappers run inside. 'Look, there's Josh at the window!' Amy hissed.

'He's trying to get out!' Holly said.

The other man started to poke in among the trees. 'He'll see Josh,' said Amy. 'I'll shout—'

Holly interrupted her. 'No, they know you! Hey!' She stood up, out in full view, climbed on the bottom spar of the fence and yelled, 'Look out!' waving towards the trees where Josh had found the big nest.

The man turned to look up towards her.

'Over there!' shouted Holly, waving vigorously to keep the man looking her way. The fence wobbling underneath her gave her an idea. 'Lie flat, Amy!' she muttered.

'What?' Amy gaped at her.

'Lie down! Now! Do it!' As Amy caught her urgency and flattened herself under the bush, Holly gritted her teeth, leaned forward and bounced. Hard.

The fence collapsed with a rending crash on to the top terrace. Holly screamed as she fell, and kept on yelling. This should cover just about any noise Josh made. Even Amy couldn't make more noise than this!

Josh heard Holly shouting and saw Bill running up the garden towards her. *Go!* he yelled silently to himself.

He shoved the window up. It only opened about thirty centimetres before it stuck. There was no time to force it open any wider. He stood on the bed, and swung one leg out—

And jammed.

A wasp stung him. He jumped violently, and his hips slid over the frame to the sill outside. He'd no time to worry about wasps now. The other leg slid out. His chest scraped through, and then his head.

There was a key turning in the lock! He desperately pulled down the window again, and jumped, backwards, blind. The cement path wasn't far below . . .

He'd seen a TV programme once about a girl who broke her neck falling three inches . . .

His feet hit the path, and he rolled flat on to his back.

He had a bumped elbow and bottom but no sprained or broken ankles. Or neck. He was all right!

As he scrambled up a big man in blue overalls with a veil over his face came around the corner of the house. It must be Archie's mate Bobo – and if Josh was speaking to him, it would look as if he'd been with him all the time! *Talk about luck!* he thought.

Above his head, Josh could hear somebody at the

window. He wanted to look up, but he didn't. He just beckoned the man over towards the tree with the wasps' nest in it. 'Er – the big one's in here.'

At the tree, while Bobo grunted with satisfaction and turned his spray on again, Josh risked a sideways glance. Two faces were frowning at the window, but there were no shouts, no panic.

He looked up the slope of terraces. At the top of the garden, Bill was helping Holly to her feet. She had saved him!

Holly didn't have to pretend to be hurt; jagged fir branches had ripped her shirt and scratched one arm badly, and the rocks of the terrace wall had bruised and scraped her bare legs. But Josh was out, and safe. It had been worth it.

'Are you OK?' the man was asking.

Holly sniffed, and wiped her nose with the back of her hand. 'More or less.' She inspected a big graze on her shin. 'Rather less than more! But it's all skin, none of it's deep.'

Act normally, Holly thought. She gazed up at the wrecked fence. There was no sign of Amy. 'Oh, dear, what a mess!' Holly exclaimed. 'I'm sorry! But I thought the wasps would get you! There's a huge nest in the trees down there.'

'How do you know?' Bill eyed her suspiciously. 'You can't see it from up here!'

'No – my pal Janet showed me it yesterday.' Thinking fast, Holly pointed to the house next door. 'She lives in there. I was coming to tell your wasp men, and then I saw you by the trees, and I thought you were going to stick your head right into it! So I shouted.'

The man seemed to accept it, Holly was glad to see. 'Better get off home, then, and get all that seen to,' he advised her.

She glanced down. 'Yes. I need a bath in antiseptic! And I'll get dad to come and mend your fence for you. He'll come over about it when he gets home from work.'

'No, that's OK, that's OK! No bother.' Bill shrugged. 'That house is empty anyway, and my friends are just renting this one. It's no skin off anybody's nose if the owners pay for it, eh?'

Holly couldn't resist it. She pointed. 'Just skin off my legs!' Amy would have been proud of that one!

To Holly's satisfaction, the man laughed almost as loudly as she did. She climbed up over the broken fence, and marched off up the path openly, turning to wave at the house corner.

As soon as he turned away, she ducked among the bushes. Phew!

A moment later, Amy crept up beside her. 'That was great, Holly!' she whispered. 'I couldn't have done better myself! Are you all right?'

'Yes, just a bit winded! Did you see what happened to Josh?'

'He's talking to the other wasp man. They can't suspect him at all, I think! Here!' Amy offered her friend something. 'I brought some chocolate – you deserve it!'

Bill looked hard at Josh as he walked back down towards the house, but Josh made sure he was busy helping Bobo with the spray. Just then, Archie came waddling out of the back door. Mr Gillingham followed him, frowning and looking up nervously.

'Where did you get to, Josh?' Archie puffed. 'I thought you were inside with me.'

To Josh's satisfaction, Bobo answered him. 'We were sorting out that nest in the trees. Now, what about that lot up there?' He gestured to the circling wasps by the window.

'They could be up in the eaves, or inside the walls, or under your floor, even. But we'll hunt them out for you!' Archie told Mr Gillingham confidently.

Mr Gillingham looked alarmed. 'No! No, there's no need for you to get in.'

'Just spray outside here. That'll do, surely!' Bill declared.

'No problem! It's all part o' the service, mate!' Archie assured him jovially. He turned to Josh. 'Here, Josh, make yourself useful. Run over to the van and get my stethoscope.' He nodded to Mr Gillingham. 'It works like a charm. You get every sound! You can hear the little beggars rustling about behind the plaster, clear as Tube trains.'

Josh edged away. 'I don't know where it is, Archie,' he said doubtfully.

'Some apprentice you are!' Archie exclaimed. 'Bobo, squirt them outside for me, while I show Josh where things are.' He clapped Josh on the back and drew him away to the van in front of the house.

As soon as they were out of sight, Josh looked at his watch, and was surprised to find it was after eleven. 'Look, Archie,' he said, 'I've got to go.' He had to get to the police as quickly as he could! And then he'd really have a story to tell his Dad.

'OK, son,' Archie puffed, beaming. 'You've been a good help, so you have. Here!' He held out a couple of pound coins.

'Oh, no!' Josh protested. 'I enjoyed it – and it was very useful. Thanks. No, really.' He backed way, grinning and shaking his head as Archie tried to give him the money. At last he convinced the man that he wasn't going to take it, and Archie turned to his van.

Josh raced off along the road, up the next street and along Grove Road to the "For Sale" house, to arrive panting beside his friends.

'Well?' Holly demanded jumping up.

'Yes!' he shouted excitedly. 'I've found her!'

It only took a couple of minutes for Josh to tell the others what he had found. He showed them the necklace he'd taken as proof. It was a simple "L" on a chain. 'And we've got to get the police to get her out, pronto!' he ended.

The girls were horrified at the thought of Lucy hanging in the harness in the hole. Amy was already jumping up to get the bikes.

'Wait!' Holly whispered. She had turned for a last look at the kidnap house. 'Something's happening down there.'

They ran back to press against the side of the house. Through the gap Holly had broken in the trees, they could see quite clearly.

Samantha Gillingham had opened the boot of the car. The two men were carrying out a roll of blanket. A long roll. The way they carried it showed it was heavy, and it sagged and bent in significant places.

'It's her! Lucy!' Josh whispered. 'It must be. They're scared Archie will find her!'

The men heaved their burden into the boot of the car, bending and shoving until it all fitted in.

'What are they doing?' Amy wondered. 'Just leaving her in the car there until Archie goes away?'

'No – they're getting in.' Holly started to back off. 'They're taking her somewhere else! Come on! We've got to follow them!'

'On bikes?' Josh cried, but Holly was already running up the drive, Amy hot on her heels. They were lifting their bikes and shoving off out on to Grove Road before Josh had even reached his, and he had to pedal hard to catch up with them.

They flew down the road, Holly's and Amy's hair flying like banners in the wind. At the bottom of the hill Amy's brakes screeched as they slowed, peering round the corner.

'There it is!' Amy yelled. The inconspicuous dark blue car was nosing out from the end of Orangery Crescent, and turning away from them.

It pulled away from them as the road went uphill again. 'Where's it going at the junction?' Amy puffed.

'Left again,' Holly reported. 'Towards the Industrial Estate!'

'Got him!' Josh gasped behind them. 'I knew it! I knew I'd seen that other man – Bill – somewhere before!'

'I thought so too!' Holly yelled.

'Who is he? Hurry up!' shouted Amy.

'I'm hurrying as fast as I can!' Josh protested, but he was pedalling too hard to argue. 'On the TV last night! He's that sculptor – the one Lucy was going to visit. Bill Gibbs!'

'Yes, that's right! That's him!' panted Holly. 'That's how they knew when she was coming! He's in on it! So they'll be going to his workshop, maybe, to hide Lucy again!'

'We'd better slow down, in case we scare them,' Amy gasped.

'Too late!' yelled Josh. They had reached the entrance to the estate just in time to see the blue car turn on to the road where they knew the sculptor's workshop was situated. But ahead of them a big white car with the police checker-board markings was driving quietly towards them. The brake lights of the blue car had come on; but as they watched, it accelerated again, passing the sculptor's unit and heading away.

'We've got to follow it!' Holly called. 'Come on, Amy! Josh—'

'I'll tell the police!' Josh yelled after her. He braked and waved desperately to the police car to stop.

Pedalling like fury, Holly and Amy chased the kidnappers' car. It was out of sight.

'It's got to turn on to the High Street!' Holly screeched over her shoulder. 'But we'll never catch it before the lights!'

'This way!' Amy shouted. She put on a spurt and led Holly on to a footpath that crossed the open ground between two units. On the far side they could squeeze their bikes between two corner posts of a fence, then remount and head up a lane towards the High Street ahead.

'There they are!' Holly pointed. 'Just ahead, at the traffic lights.'

Cars jammed the High Street, waiting to get along to the lights. There wasn't a spare inch to squeeze the bikes through.

The pavement was crowded, but quite wide here. 'Come on! We've got to!' Holly called.

Angry shoppers shouted at the girls as they wriggled their bikes among the crowd, but they got on quite well, for a bit.

Unluckily, it was a fine day. The Pot-Luck Cafe had put tables out on the pavement. The girls had to go back on to the road about fifty metres short of the lights.

The lights turned green. Holly stood on her pedals to look ahead. 'They've turned left, up Union Street!'

'This way!' Amy shot off to the side, up a shopping arcade.

They skidded among furiously yelling pedestrians, children jumping, a boy on a skateboard, a pram and two pushchairs and a poodle yapping on a lead. Then they shot through a fire exit passage at the far end, and down a flight of steps. 'Yaa-a-a-a-a-agh!' Amy screamed in excitement as she bumped down them. They swung round six huge wheelie bins, through a gap between two shops and out on to Union Street.

There was the blue car, held up in a queue of traffic at road works just ahead.

'We can't keep this up!' Amy puffed as they worked their way up between the cars. 'They'll be on the open road in a minute! What should we do?'

'Hang on!' Holly stopped behind a lorry, gasping. Her voice was muffled, as she was rummaging about in her saddlebags. In a moment, she straightened up and offered something to Amy. 'Blow this up and tie it before the lights change! Hurry up!'

It was a red balloon.

Amy wanted to ask what it was for, but Holly was busy getting something else out. Amy drew a deep breath and puffed as hard as she could.

'Not too tight!' Holly panted. 'It mustn't burst! Oh, there's the green light! Come on, Amy!'

Frantically, Amy tied off the balloon, gripped it in her teeth and followed Holly belting off along the road. She was still baffled.

'This way!' Holly led Amy straight along the inside edge of the ditch that was being dug in the road. They bounced over ridges and piles of rubble, past the workmen shouting at them, and reached the far end of the road works a bit ahead of the big lorry that had hidden them before, but by the time they reached the next set of traffic lights down the road, it had overtaken them again.

Holly caught hold of the corner of the lorry to steady herself while she stood up and looked forward past it. 'Yes! They're just at the traffic lights – they'll be away first! We've got to go now!'

'What do I do?' Amy asked.

Holly grabbed the balloon. 'They know you. So go and park your bike beside their car, on the inside, and keep them looking at you. Go on!'

Amy still didn't know what Holly was going to do, but there wasn't time to ask, not if she was going to reach the kidnappers' car before the lights changed.

She did better than just parking beside the blue car. She scraped her bike right along the paintwork and drew up with a screech of her brakes.

There was a shout of annoyance from inside the car, and the window rolled down. 'What on earth do you think you're doing!' Bill Gibbs shouted.

Amy bent down to look into the car. 'Sorry!' she said, trying to hide her panting. 'Looks like I've scraped your paint – but it's just a scratch! Oh, it's you, Samantha! I seem to have done it again, eh? Sorry!'

'You again!' Mr Gillingham was furious. 'What the devil are you doing here?'

'No need to swear at me!' Amy protested indignantly.

On the other side of the car Holly had the balloon in one hand. In the other, she held a few inches torn off the roll of Sellotape, forgotten at the bottom of her saddlebag after showing the conjuring trick to her friends. She reached over, bent the car aerial down, and quickly but firmly fastened the balloon on to the end with the Sellotape.

Samantha was looking suspicious. 'I haven't seen her around before, and now here she is twice in two days!' she snapped. The kidnappers stared at Amy through the car window.

Holly straightened up. Mr Gillingham saw the movement out of the corner of his eye and looked round. But he didn't know Holly. She didn't glance down; she just stood quietly beside her bike, not looking at Amy or at the car.

The lights had changed, and the traffic behind was hooting. The blue car shot away.

At last, Amy could see what Holly had been doing. She started to yell with delight.

The brilliant red balloon, bobbing high above the traffic, marked the kidnappers' car out to everybody within half a mile. And the kidnappers knew nothing about it!

Holly wheeled her bike towards the pavement through a gap in the traffic.

Amy reached for her, and then stopped.

But Holly grinned. 'Go ahead!' she said.

The two of them hugged each other and danced round the pavement shouting with glee, while everybody in the passing cars laughed at them, and they didn't care!

10

Round-up

Holly and Amy had just stopped, gasping for breath, when a police car drew up beside them. Josh poked his head out of the window anxiously. 'Did you lose them?' he demanded.

'No!' Amy shouted. 'Holly's marked them!'

The policewoman driving the car was grinning as her partner radioed their news to the station.

'Balloon! What'll you think of next? But we'll stop them,' she said confidently.

Her partner looked round from his radio. 'Inspector Ross says if this is another false alarm he'll have your guts for garters.'

'He didn't!' Holly exclaimed.

'In those very words!' The policeman was emphatic.

'But it's true!' Josh assured them. 'That necklace proves it! And the red hair!'

'Don't tell me, tell the Inspector!' the policeman said. 'But that's certainly why he's taking this chance on you again. We have orders to take you in to the station.'

'I can't get three bikes in the boot,' the driver said. 'Have you got a cycle chain? Fasten those bikes to the traffic lights, and climb in.'

Holly did as she was instructed and she and Amy climbed into the back seat beside Josh.

They were only halfway to the police station when the radio squawked again, and the policeman turned round, grinning broadly. 'Well done, you three! They've stopped the car, and found Lucy Ogilvie safe and sound! Well done!'

Over the din of Holly, Josh and Amy cheering in the back, he told his partner, 'We've to take the kids in to the Highgate Infirmary. Miss Ogilvie insists she wants to meet the boy who found her.' Nodding, the policewoman turned the car towards the hospital.

They had to wait for half an hour, while doctors

checked that Lucy was as well as she said she was. Josh used the time to phone his father, and tell him what they had been doing. 'We'll be home soon, dad,' he said.

'Soon?' his father repeated. 'You don't know the police! I'll phone the Adamses and the Hunts, and we'll come and collect you, or you'll be making statements for hours! But, son—' He paused. '—I'm proud of you. All three of you!'

Josh felt ready to burst with happiness.

When he got back to the waiting-room, Inspector Ross was just coming down the corridor from the wards. He smiled at them, and held up his hands in surrender. 'OK, you were right! I admit it!'

'That's OK, Inspector,' Amy chirped. 'You just didn't know the K.I.D.Z.!'

'Oh, Amy!' Holly said, exasperated. She smiled at the Inspector. 'We're glad it's turned out all right.'

'Yes,' Josh agreed. 'Our parents will be coming for us soon, Inspector.'

'Right,' the Inspector nodded. 'I'll have to go – I've a set of suspects to question! You can come in to the station to give a statement this afternoon. OK?'

'OK,' they chorused, and he hurried out with a grin.

A nurse came into the waiting-room. 'Are you three the rescuers?' she asked, smiling at them. 'Miss Ogilvie says will you come in. But you've only got one minute; she's had a sedative to help her sleep.'

They followed her to a small private ward, where Lucy lay, pale and tired, with her father beside her, holding her hand as if he was scared to let her go.

Mr Ogilvie was as pale as his daughter and looked quite exhausted, but he was smiling too. He stood up and came round the bed to shake Holly's, Amy's and Josh's hands, one after the other. 'Thank you. Oh, thank you! Thank you so much!' He didn't seem to be able to think of anything else to say.

'You're the ones they call the K.I.D.Z., the policeman said,' Lucy murmured. 'Tell me who you are, please.'

Blushing slightly, they gave her their names and shook her hand, Josh last. She smiled at him, and put her hand up to her head. 'Wasn't it you that found me? And pulled out my hair?'

'That was me,' Josh admitted. 'I'm sorry – but I couldn't think of anything else that would prove I'd actually found you. Sorry!'

'Don't apologise!' she said faintly. She laughed a little. 'I'd rather go completely bald than have stayed there!'

The nurse came in. 'I'm going to shoo you all out now,' she declared firmly. 'Yes, even you, Mr Ogilvie. Lucy must rest. You can talk outside.'

'Hold on a second,' Lucy whispered, grasping Josh's hand. 'Dad, the kidnappers told me about the reward you offered. You're going to give it to them, aren't you?'

'Of course!' Mr Ogilvie assured her. 'I was ready to offer ten times as much, to get you back!'

'Don't let us stop you!' Amy said brightly.

'Amy!' Holly grumbled under her breath. Sometimes her friend was *too* much!

'I want to give you each something personal,' Lucy said sleepily. 'Just from me, to show how grateful I am to you – to you all! What would you like?'

The K.I.D.Z. looked at one another. 'Josh could do with a Swiss Army Knife with scissors, so that he doesn't have to scalp the next person we rescue,' said Amy.

'Holly should get another magic set, for herself, not for Jamie. That was what helped us, more than anything,' Josh suggested.

Holly grinned. 'And we all know what Amy would love! A whole freezerful of choc-ices!'

Everyone laughed, and looked to see if Lucy was laughing too; but she was asleep.

Quietly, the K.I.D.Z. tiptoed out.

Look out for more K.I.D.Z. adventures!

Treasure Hunt

A suitcase full of money – stolen, then lost!
But not for long now Holly, Amy and Josh
are on the trail. The K.I.D.Z. are ready to
follow every lead there is...